W9-AKY-406

DISCARD

Onondaga Free Library
4840 West Seneca Turnpike
Syracuse, NY 13215
315-492-1727
www.oflibrary.org

Thirteen Chairs

DISCARD

Also by Dave Shelton

A Boy and a Bear in a Boat

Thirteen Chairs

Dave Shelton

David Fickling Books

SCHOLASTIC INC. / NEW YORK

ONONDAGA FREE

Text copyright © 2015 and illustrations copyright © 2014 by Dave Shelton

All rights reserved. Published by Scholastic Inc., *Publishers since 1920*, by arrangement with David Fickling Books, Oxford, England. SCHOLASTIC and associated logos are trademarks and/or registered trademarks of Scholastic Inc. DAVID FICKLING BOOKS and associated logos are trademarks and/or registered trademarks of David Fickling Books.

First published in the United Kingdom in 2014 by David Fickling Books, 31 Beaumont Street, Oxford, OX1 2NP.
www.davidficklingbooks.com

The publisher does not have any control over and does not assume any responsibility for author or third-party websites or their content.

No part of this publication may be reproduced, stored in a retrieval system, or transmitted in any form or by any means, electronic, mechanical, photocopying, recording, or otherwise, without written permission of the publisher. For information regarding permission, write to Scholastic Inc., Attention: Permissions Department, 557 Broadway, New York, NY 10012.

This book is a work of fiction. Names, characters, places, and incidents are either the product of the author's imagination or are used fictitiously, and any resemblance to actual persons, living or dead, business establishments, events, or locales is entirely coincidental.

Library of Congress Cataloging-in-Publication Data

Shelton, Dave, author.
Thirteen chairs / by Dave Shelton.—[First U.S. edition].
pages cm
First published in the United Kingdom in 2014 by David Fickling Books.
Summary: When Jack enters the deserted house in his neighborhood, he finds a group of people who invite him to take the thirteenth chair in the room and share a story—in the house where the ghosts meet.
ISBN 978-0-545-81665-6
1. Haunted houses—Juvenile fiction. 2. Storytelling—Juvenile fiction. 3. Death—Juvenile fiction. 4. Ghost stories. [1. Haunted houses—Fiction. 2. Storytelling—Fiction. 3. Death—Fiction. 4. Ghosts—Fiction.] I. Title.
PZ7.S54147Th 2015
823.92—dc23
[Fic]
2014035628

10 9 8 7 6 5 4 3 2 1   15 16 17 18 19

Printed in the U.S.A.   23

First edition, August 2015

Book design by Ness Wood

For Tim, Joanne, Emily, Sam, Noah, and Freya

J ack stands in the dark on the landing of the old house, and looks at his feet. He is outside the last of three doors, the one that is underlined with flickering light. He doesn't move. He stares down at the twin crescents of light reflecting on the toes of his shoes. He looks at the thin highlights along the edges of the bare floorboards and at the pattern of the grain in the wood in the pale puddle of light that leaks under the door. He has been here for minutes, his hand on the door handle, debating whether or not to go in. Common sense insists that he must not, because there is no way of knowing what might be inside. But curiosity insists the opposite, for the same reason.

And Jack is a curious boy.

So he holds a breath behind clamped lips, turns the handle, and goes in. And there they are, twelve of them, sitting around a big circular wooden table and looking at him as the door creaks loudly to announce his arrival. It takes him a moment to see them properly— the room is only dimly lit by candles, but after the darkness outside it still seems bright—and it takes his eyes some time to adjust. When they do, and the indistinct figures settle into focus, it is the pale man, farthest from Jack, whom he notices first.

He is a small man, soberly dressed in a dark suit that is neatly tailored and primly buttoned, a crisp white shirt with a wing collar, and a plain dark tie. His hair is short and well behaved. His posture is excellent. He is neat and tidy and quiet. There is nothing about him, his slightly old-fashioned clothes aside, to mark him out as extraordinary, and yet he exudes a quiet authority that draws Jack's eye. His face is lit from below by the candle on the table in front of him, giving it that torch-under-the-chin spooky effect, but his measured smile is reassuring.

"You're late," says one of the others, one of the women over to the right, her voice scratchy and irritated.

"We're *all* late," says another.

Jack doesn't understand what she means, but he's grateful that she sounds friendly. Looks it, too, when he turns his head to see. She has an attractive smile, which she must have used a lot judging by the laugh lines on her face, and she watches Jack with wry amusement, her dark eyes glinting in the candlelight, short silver-gray hair shining.

"Come on in, then," she says, raising an arm and beckoning with long fingers, tickling at the air. "No skulking in the dark. Over here where we can see you." Her voice is a soft and lovely thing, round and warm with a sweet tang of teasing laughter. Jack does as he is told and steps three sleepwalking paces into the room as the door creaks shut behind him.

It is a large room, with high ceilings, bare wooden floors, and empty walls. The only light comes from the candles on the table, one for each of those seated there, casting shifting, looming shadows onto the crumbling plaster of the walls. There is one large window, off to Jack's left, with long pale curtains pulled not quite completely closed across it. Jack remembers himself a few minutes ago, outside on the gravel drive, looking up at the thin vertical line of light at the window, and shivering at the small thrill of fear that it gave him.

"You *will* be joining us," says the pale man, and it doesn't sound like a question, though Jack answers anyway.

"Yes."

"We'll need another chair," says the pale man in a soft, calm voice. "Lee, could you, please?"

There are children in the two nearest seats: a boy, a few years older than Jack, and a girl, a little younger. The boy rises from his seat. He is tall, and he'd be taller still if he stood up straight, but he does not. He stoops, as if embarrassed by his own height, and he bows his head shyly, his mop of hair hiding his eyes.

"Sure," he mumbles. "I'll go and, um . . ." He pulls out his own chair and indicates it with a fuzzy gesture of his hand. "Here, have mine and I'll . . ."

"Thanks," says Jack and, almost without thinking, sits down. He hears the door creaking open and then shut behind him once again.

"Welcome," says the pale man. "You are welcome."

He is more or less directly across the table from Jack, who stares at him with what he knows must be a ridiculous grin on his face, so tight and tense it threatens to shatter his teeth. The pale man is a full head shorter than either of his neighbors, yet somehow his is the more powerful presence. It's difficult to know how old he is. He might be thirty or he might be sixty. There are no obvious signs of advancing age: no hair loss, no graying, very few lines or wrinkles. But there is something about him, in his eyes perhaps, that suggests more years lived, more experience, more sadness.

Jack is still working hard on trying to appear relaxed when he hears the door again. He looks around to see the stooping boy, Lee, enter, carrying a chair.

"Excuse . . . can I just . . . ?" Jack shifts his chair a little to the right, and three bearded men seated beyond Lee all shuffle left a little, and Lee apologetically slides the thirteenth chair into place at Jack's side and folds himself down onto it. "Oh, and . . ." He places a candle on the table in front of Jack and the girl lights it from her own, her grin highlighted in the light of the flame, her eyes thrilled wide.

"Thank you, Lee," says the pale man. "Thank you, Amelia." Then he turns his attention back to Jack. "And you are . . . ?"

"Oh! Yes. Sorry. Jack," says Jack.

"Jack. Good. Welcome." His eyes are still and dark, each with a twisting worm of reflected candlelight

4

dancing on its surface. "Let me introduce you." He raises one hand just barely off the other and turns its thin fingers the smallest amount to gesture toward the stooping boy at Jack's left-hand side.

"Lee," says the pale man, and Lee bows his low head even lower in acknowledgment.

"Mr. Blackmore," says the pale man, continuing clockwise around the table. "Piotr, Mr. Harlow." These are the three bearded men in a row, but Jack only really takes in Piotr in the middle. He is enormous. He looks as if he might have been carved from a mountain. From within his extravagant rust-and-ashes beard there appears a wide and welcoming grin of crooked teeth.

"Ha! Jack! Is very good meeting you! Yes!" He raises his impossibly large hands aloft in a gesture of welcome that only just falls short of smacking each of his neighbors in the face.

"Mr. Fowler," says the pale man, and the fellow seated to his right gives a deep, slow nod. If Piotr has been carved from stone then this man's features are etched in wood. He has an angular, bony face that is weathered like ancient timbers: salted and windblown and ragged and worn. He looks as if he has seen more than his share of troubles, but for all that his mouth and eyes are smiling now as he dips his head in Jack's direction.

"Mr. Randolph," says the pale man, and raises the fingers of his left hand now, and the fellow on that side stiffly nods.

5

"Miss Crane," says the pale man.

"Frances," says Miss Crane, the friendly woman with the short gray hair and the laugh lines. "Hello, Jack." She smiles that warm smile again.

"Professor Cleary, Mrs. Trent, Miss Mulligan."

"*Ms.* Mulligan," says the last, a smartly dressed young woman with a determined haircut.

Frances smiles and mutters, "You tell him, Katy."

"And Amelia," says the pale man, ignoring them both.

The young girl to Jack's right points a curious stare at him that would be disturbingly intense even if it were not magnified by the thick lenses of her spectacles.

"Very pleased to meet you, Jack. Thank you very much," she says quickly, in a blank tone, as if reciting the words from a script without any understanding of their meaning.

"Hello," says Jack, leaning away from her continuing stare, and then turning his attention back to the pale man, expecting him at last to introduce himself. But he does not. He stares placidly back at Jack, and once again Jack's attention is entirely drawn to him, as if the rest of the room has somehow dimmed.

"Very good," says the pale man, with the tiniest nod of his head, then he places the one hand back on top of the other. "Shall we begin?"

Begin what? wonders Jack.

But he likes not knowing. He's always liked not knowing what will happen next. He really shouldn't be here, for all kinds of reasons. He has no idea who any of these people are, and he's heard the rumors, of course: the things that are meant to happen here. There was a boy who told him all about it ages ago. Amazing stories. He doesn't believe them for a second, but still, he can't help feeling a little scared.

At least he's closest to the door, so if he decides he needs to get out in a hurry then he can. He's a fast runner. Faster than any of this lot anyway, he reckons. So he's nervous, but not too nervous. Not quite so much that it overcomes his curiosity. Not quite so afraid that he'll give up on finding out what happens next.

"Mr. Blackmore," says the pale man, keeping his head perfectly still and turning only his eyes to face the man he is addressing. The man sitting next to stooping Lee, the nearest to Jack of the three bearded men, has a shaved head, and is dressed all in black. His beard, a carefully shaped, neat enclosure around his mouth, is black, too. He looks up, turns his head in the pale man's direction.

"Yes."

"Perhaps you might take the first turn?"

"Yes, of course." Mr. Blackmore turns his head back to face front, purses his lips as he gathers himself. His nostrils flare as he takes a deep breath, and another.

Jack wonders what's coming, and tries to look as if he already knows.

Then it turns out that one part of the rumors is true, because what happens next is that Mr. Blackmore tells a story.

Let Me Sleep

I t began in the marketplace.

William Cobb liked markets because crowds were very helpful to him. His work was easiest where people were closely gathered together, where a little accidental jostling was perfectly usual, and a clumsy collision could quite distract you from the lightest touch of his nimble, slender fingers relieving you of your purse or your watch. There was a better choice of victims in a crowd, too, and people brought their money with them on market day.

The sturdy, young, fair-haired man in the leather waistcoat, though, was not the type who would usually spark William's interest. He knew what to look for to identify a worthwhile victim, and this young fellow showed very little promise. He looked poor. His simple clothes were clean enough but showing their age: his shirt a little frayed at the cuffs, his trousers at the knees and hems. What is more, he looked alert and strong. So the possible gains from robbing him were slight, but the risk of getting caught, and probably severely beaten for his troubles, was high. And yet for some reason, William did not immediately search for easier pickings. Something about the young man held his attention and provoked in him a strange sense of dislike. The man

11

was buying flowers. Oh, so he was undoubtedly *in love*, and these were a gift for his sweetheart, no doubt. How sickening.

The young man took a coin from his purse and bought a very modest posy—all he could afford, probably. Then, as the young man accepted his change, William spotted a glint of gold from his left hand. A sly glance as the young lover waved good-bye to the flower girl confirmed this to be a wedding band. The young man strode away, grinning contentedly, and now seemed so unspeakably happy that William felt it virtually a duty to rob him. He would deprive him of his wedding ring at the earliest opportunity. It was, William was sure, the only thing of any real value that he possessed, so taking it would be all the sweeter.

So William followed him, observing the young man with a keen eye, noting anything that might prove useful in his task. He was quite brilliant at picking pockets: a master of the craft, with the sly, quick hands of a conjuror. To take a ring directly from a finger without detection, though, that was a more difficult task. But if he could invent some excuse to shake the young man's hand then it might be managed, he thought, if the ring was not too tight.

The young man's business in the market was swiftly concluded. He bought a spade, after much indecision and a good deal of tiresomely good-natured haggling, and then took himself away by foot along a lane out of the town.

William followed him, some way behind, awaiting the best moment to make his move. The lane itself was too busy, too full of witnesses, but as it took a turn to loop around the base of a hill, the young man left it to set off along a footpath that led up past the woodland at the crown of the hill.

Keeping his distance, William followed the young man as he dawdled uphill, whistling happily as he went. William hated that. He really would have to put a stop to it. He had devised a plan, but for it to work he needed to approach his victim face-on. He left the path and ducked off, still unobserved, into the woods and raced through it, at what he hoped was a safe distance from the path, until he judged he must be well ahead of his prey. Then he turned out of the woods, found the path again and, walking slowly now, headed back along it. He soon came to a point where the path turned sharply around the edge of the woodland. He stopped a few paces short of the corner and waited.

Once the approaching whistling grew loud enough that its owner must be about to appear, William set off walking quickly down to meet him. As the young man appeared around the corner, William feigned surprise as he collided with him, knocking him off his feet. The newly acquired spade clanged to the ground as its hapless buyer thudded down on his backside in a patch of wildflowers. William stood over him, offering his left hand to the dazed young man to help him back up.

"Oh, I'm so sorry," said William. "I didn't hear you coming and then, I'm afraid, I must have tripped. Are you all right, my dear sir? What must you think of me?" And by the time he had hauled the fellow upright again, the ring had slipped easily from its owner's finger into William's helping hand. It was beautifully done. It was all William could do to stop himself from grinning at the artistry of it. To conceal his glee, he stooped to pick up the fallen spade.

"Oh, no harm done." The young man's fall had apparently not knocked any of the innocent joy from him. His boyish grin persisted even as he swatted away a bee that had been disturbed from the flowers. William grinned back at him, at least until the bee came his way. It was flying straight into his face so, his right hand still being gripped around the spade, he raised his left to swipe at the creature with an open palm.

He realized his mistake at once, but there was nothing he could do about it. The ring fell to the ground. It struck a stone with a piercing metallic note that seemed to resonate for an eternity. The young man's big, open, honest face gazed down at it in bemusement, then up at William full of sad betrayal. Without a thought William swung the spade hard at his head, and the man dropped like a felled oak.

William waited a moment, the spade held ready to strike again, but the young man lay still where he had fallen. There was something unnatural about how his neck was twisted so far around. And his chest was still.

William was sure that the blow had not been enough to kill him, but somehow he had contrived to break his neck as he fell. He was dead. This was very inconsiderate of him. But at least he had provided William with a spade.

He dragged the body away into the woods, and there dug as deep a grave as he could manage, and buried it. He scattered leaves and twigs over the freshly turned earth and then, because it amused him, the flowers from the market. He dropped the spade a good distance from the grave, rejoined the footpath, and walked quickly on. He did not stop until, past dusk, he took a room at the inn in the village he had by then reached, a safe distance from the scene of his crime.

Two days after that he was in the next county; a week later, in Norwich. There was a man there whom he had known for many years, though neither of them knew the other's name, and William sold to him the spoils of his recent endeavors. He kept hold of the ring, though. Even so, he had had a profitable time of it in the previous weeks, and found himself temporarily wealthy as a result of the sale.

For the next few days, William set about the task of lightening the load in his purse. He took a good room at a coaching inn, ate well, drank heavily, gambled, and indulged the company of a great number of friends, some of whom he could not actually recall knowing. But he didn't especially care. He was having a fine time of it, and the recent brief unpleasantness was altogether forgotten. So much so that, one night, back in his lodgings with a full belly and a light head, he happened to pick up the stolen ring, and it took him a moment to remember where it had come from.

When he did remember, he felt no remorse. He held the ring up in the candlelight and briefly enjoyed the tiny dance of the reflected flame. It was a fine little trinket. He should get a good price for it when he did decide to sell it. Distractedly, he tried it on. It was a good fit. Then he fell asleep in his chair.

When it came it was so quiet it was barely a sound at all, less than a whisper. But William heard the words clearly enough; and thought, as well, that he felt a wisp of breath against his ear.

Give it back.

Terror jolted him awake with a sharp cry that blew out his candle and dropped him into darkness.

"Who's there?" he cried. He fumbled for matches, spilled most of them, and took three attempts to finally strike one. He held it high, trembling and twitching, as he turned two full circles on the spot, staring into the dimly revealed room. Finding no one there, he relit the candle and looked again. Nobody.

He cursed his foolishness, and his dreams, and made his way to bed, singing to himself—quite without thinking—a song from his childhood. He lit a second candle from the first, then climbed into the bed and, shivering at a chill he hadn't previously noticed, drew the blankets up tight and listened attentively to the silence. Satisfied that he was most definitely alone, his grip upon the bedclothes gradually loosened and the tension in his body unwound. He closed his eyes, and his thoughts began to dissolve as sleep embraced him.

Give it back.

The voice was just as quiet and as clear. William's eyes snapped open, but he was still alone. He trembled and shook. He knew the voice now. It was the voice of a dead man buried in a wood. He tried to convince himself he had been dreaming, but he knew that he had not.

He took off the ring and shut it away in a drawer, but he did not sleep again that night. He did not hear the voice again, but he did not—could not—sleep.

Sometime before dawn, he rose, dressed, and, without much thought, gathered together his most valuable and most necessary possessions into a satchel, and left the house. The ring, he left in the drawer: he wanted no part of it now. He walked out to the city limits with no idea where he was going, and when buildings gave way to countryside and farmland he still carried on, and on. He walked at a good pace, and without rest or sustenance, through the dawn, through the day, and through village after village until, after dusk, with no idea where he might be, he crept into a barn on some remote farm.

He collapsed to the floor and pulled straw around and over him for a blanket. He didn't even notice the hardness of the ground, felt nothing but gratitude for the opportunity to rest now. His feet ached, the muscles in his legs burned, and he felt drained and hollow. But he was pleased to be so many miles from his lodgings, away from the ring and the dead man's voice, and exhaustion would surely now send him quickly to sleep. Blissful, beautiful sleep. His eyelids fell shut.

Give it back.

No! How could this be? William screwed his eyes tighter shut and tried to ignore the voice. He wrapped his arms around his head, covering his ears. It made no difference.

Give it back.

Louder now. More insistent.

This was madness. This was imagination. This was the fevered invention of his mind, addled by lack of sleep and desperate exhaustion.

Give it back.

William yelled out. But his voice had been silent for over a day and he was unable to form actual words, his mind too maddened and panicked to form thoughts to demand them, he could only let out a strange animal sound of profound anguish. Then the tears came, and he did not hear the voice anymore, only his own racking sobs, and he lay there, weeping like a child, until morning. And then he staggered to his feet and walked on.

William kept walking for two more days, but all the distance he put between himself and the ring made no difference. He could not escape the whispering voice.

And despite a weariness far beyond any he had ever known before, he still could not rest. The voice, or just the thought of the voice, held him back from the brink of sleep, denying him the thing he most craved.

He was *so* tired, so utterly ragged and broken, that it was now a kind of madness. His thoughts were small, angry things that flitted and lurched and tumbled and fought each other in his head. And though he could not sleep, he began at times to think that he *was* dreaming. All that he saw seemed unreal, distorted, and terrifying.

People were the worst, so he avoided all human contact, but still he was never truly alone. Every step was full of pain, and his muscles seemed to have worn away, and his limbs had grown heavy and clumsy. He felt as if he didn't know how his body worked anymore. And the one thought he could hold on to, the one constant, like a screaming hunger beyond any hunger he had ever known, was his desperate need to rest, to sleep, to stop.

On that third night, hunched up at the foot of a tree, shaking with madness, he pleaded with the dead man, crying out to the night: "Let me sleep! For the love of God, please, let me sleep!"

And the voice replied: *Give it back. Give it back and let* me *sleep!*

William, blank-faced, gave a weary nod. He rose unsteadily to his feet and began to walk back the way he had come.

*

Standing at the open drawer, William looked down at the ring. He felt nothing. He reached down, picked it up, and placed it on the same finger as before. Then he went out and paid all the money he still had for one further coach journey. It was a long trip and William stared out of the window for all the hours that it took, the chaos in his head fractionally tamed by his new sense of purpose, his glimmer of hope.

In the woods on the hill it took some time to find the spade again, but then he returned to the grave as if led to it. The remains of the flowers confirmed that this was the place; he noticed the sickly-sweet smell of their decay as he started to dig.

The ground was mercifully soft. He had no strength left in his weary limbs, but a desperate will still somehow moved them, and slowly he progressed down into the earth. His body ached, but he did not notice. Tears fell from his eyes, but he did not know it. His breath rasped in time with the rhythm of his work.

When he reasoned that he was deep enough, he knelt down at the bottom of the hole and scraped at the earth with his hands. Quite quickly he found cloth: the upper part of a shirtsleeve. He scrabbled at the soil, feverishly scratching earth away to reveal an arm, a hand. He held it for a moment, looked down at his own hands, blackened by the earth, clasped as if strangely praying around the body's cold, dead flesh. When he pulled the ring from his finger, it left a clean pink circle of flesh amid the earth-stained skin.

He lifted the dead man's hand, parted the ring finger from the others, and slid the ring onto it. Then, for a moment, he knelt there, still holding the dead man's hand, and he closed his eyes expectantly and listened to his own breathing. There was no other sound. The silence was beautiful.

William laid the dead man's hand back by the side of his body, then filled his own lungs with the sweet woodland air. He opened his eyes again, as if waking to a new day. He might have smiled if he had had the strength.

It was over.

But when he tried to rise to his feet he found that he could not. And it was not fatigue that prevented him. The dead man's hand was closed around his own, holding him down. He pulled against it wearily but it only pulled back with greater determination. He toppled forward, his face landing against soil beneath which the dead man's face must have lain. He knew he should struggle, but his slow brain was failing to tell his body how. And then he felt the embrace of another bony arm thrown around his back, holding him down with surprising force. Then the other hand released its grip, reached up above him, and began to claw at the earth, bringing down clods of it onto his back.

William made no sound, barely resisted, as the soil piled up over him. After a while, the left arm held him while the right pulled down more earth, and more.

And the weight of it was like bedclothes. And as more fell over his head, there was darkness. There was the smell of earth, and there was darkness.

He knew he must not sleep. He knew he must not. But he was so tired.

*T*hank you, Mr. Blackmore," says the pale man, and a flicker of a smile plays briefly upon Mr. Blackmore's pursed lips before he regains his solemn expression and gives a tiny nod. Then he leans forward and blows out his candle, shifts his chair away from the table, and sits back.

Jack, emerging from the spell of the story like a swimmer breaking the surface of a lake, gasps for air. It is only a tiny noise but it resonates around the otherwise silent room. Then he gulps, and that sounds deafening, too. But, looking around, no one seems to have taken any notice of him. It looks, too, as if no one else has reacted to the story quite as he has. No one else looks scared. Instead, there are smiles and nods of appreciation, as if everyone is relishing the lingering aftertaste of something delicious.

"Well told, sir," says the man with the ragged face, widely grinning. "A fine start to the proceedings. A good old-fashioned tale, eh, Mr. Osterley?"

Apparently, Mr. Osterley is the pale man. He smiles a thin smile. "Quite so, Mr. Fowler. A fine traditional tale."

"Aye, sir. You have the truth of it there, right enough. And a burial in it, too, eh?"

Mr. Osterley's face tightens just the tiniest amount.

"After a fashion," he says, and Jack wonders why there seems to be a tone of distaste in his voice now. "Perhaps we shall have a more modern tale next. Mr. Harlow, I imagine you might have something suitable?"

So that is what tonight is all about then, *thinks Jack. Ghost stories. Well, that's all right. Jack likes a good ghost story. He loves a good scare. Though he'll have to take a turn himself at some point. He'll need to give that some thought.*

Mr. Harlow, it turns out, is the man next to Mr. Fowler, and the farthest from Jack of the three bearded men. His beard is neither as neat as Mr. Blackmore's nor as substantial as the giant Piotr's. It is a scraggy mess, patchy and wild as an untended garden. He is a touch taller than average, and probably used to be handsome once, before so much of his face got hidden away. He is smiling an uneasy smile, nervous and tight. All of him seems to be too tight, in fact. He seems ill at ease, tense, and that tension seems to be pulling him out of his ideal shape. He has a notepad on the table in front of him, a cheap, shabby-looking thing, spiral-bound, tatty, and tea-stained. He flicks quickly through its pages with jerky, slender fingers.

"My story tonight is, um . . ." He has leafed through too far, to the few blank pages left at the back of the pad. Flustered, he starts at the beginning again. "I wrote it out, years ago. Just hang on a minute . . ." he says rather apologetically. "If I don't, I . . . Where is it? . . . I get rather lost and get things in the wrong . . ." His fingers come to a halt at a dense page of text full of crossings out, corrections, and amendments. He jabs a finger down at it, as if trying to pin it down and ensure

it cannot escape. "It's a story about . . . Did I ever mention that I used to be a taxi driver? Before, I mean. Well, obviously before, but . . . Uh, anyway, I was, for a while. And I heard this story once, from one of the other drivers. It's kind of about a taxi, you see, and, um . . . So, that's why I chose this one, because . . . Anyway, see what you think."

Mr. Harlow looks down at his notepad, quiet for a moment, gathering his thoughts and his courage.

Then he begins to read.

The Wrong Side of the Road

Against the background noise of heavy rain, he heard the low rumble of an engine and the crunch of tires on gravel, and he was glad of the excuse to end his telephone call.

"Got to go," he said. "Bloody taxi's here early and I don't want to risk losing him with the weather like this. I'll see you there. Bye." He put the phone down and glanced out of the window at the waiting cab. "Bloody idiot." He meant it equally for the driver and the business colleague who had just called. Two for the price of one.

He gulped down the last mouthful from his glass of whisky—an expensive single malt—and pulled on his overcoat as he walked to the front door. The black car's rear passenger door was open, ready for him, but the driver had returned to his seat rather than remain outside in the rain to usher him in and close the door after him.

No tip for you, he thought. He ducked into the backseat and slammed the door shut in what he hoped was a clearly dissatisfied manner.

"The Hardwicke Center," he said. "You know where that is, I suppose?"

The driver didn't reply. He didn't even turn his head, only raised his left hand in a vaguely reassuring wave while tapping with his right hand at the screen of his GPS. Then he eased the cab around the circular gravel drive and out toward the road.

"Turn right." The GPS's voice was female; soft and warm, but precise, too.

Sprawled in the backseat, he scowled at the back of the driver's head. *They used to just know,* he thought. *They had to learn all the routes by heart. Now they just rely on gadgets. Probably foreign, too. Too embarrassed to try to talk to me in English. Oh well, at least that might mean he won't try to start a conversation.* He'd become all too familiar with the conversations of taxi drivers in the last year or so. He didn't like talking with anyone very much, but he especially hated talking with taxi drivers.

"At the next intersection, turn left."

"Can't you turn the sound off, at least?"

He wanted silence. Actually, no, he didn't want silence. He just didn't want anything to interrupt the sounds of driving: the rain on the roof of the car, the noise of the road beneath the wheels, the thrum of the engine. He missed it. He'd loved driving. Loved his car. Oh, his beautiful car! He didn't want to think about what had happened to it. When was it? Must have been about a year ago now. He'd been so unlucky. There must have been some oil or ice or something at that corner: he never would have come off

30

otherwise, whatever the so-called experts from the police said. And he hadn't been *so* far over the limit. He'd just lost track a bit at the office party. It was difficult to judge quantities in those plastic cups.

The driver gave him the same vague wave as before, again without a word.

"In two hundred meters, turn left."

Oh, what was the use? He dug his smartphone out of his inside pocket and clicked on the calendar. Then he scrolled back in time to a year ago. Well, would you look at that? The accident had been *exactly* a year ago. To the very day! Exactly a year since he had lost his beloved new car, and his license, just because he'd had a glass or two of wine too many. And how was he supposed to know how strong that punch had been? It really wasn't fair.

"At the intersection, turn right."

He glanced out of the window, vaguely recognizing his surroundings. It was an odd route they were taking. Not the one he'd have chosen himself, but he chose not to question it. He had noticed scars on the backs of the driver's hands. Dozens of them. He didn't want to guess at how he might have gotten them, and he certainly wasn't going to ask. Instead, he returned his attention to his phone. He stared at the date and, despite himself, thought back to that night.

It had been snowing then. Prettily at first, as he had set off home, snow from a black-and-white Christmas movie. But then it had gotten worse about halfway back, and become harder to see where he was going. Perhaps he *should* have slowed down a little, but the road through the wood was always very quiet, so where was the harm? That was part of why he'd chosen to live out there in the middle of nowhere, after all. And a car like that—well, it's just not right to drive it slowly.

He closed his eyes in a moment of reverie, remembering the car. He'd only had it a couple of days. It had still had that new-car smell, not really a nice smell in itself, but full of excitement and promise. The thought of it almost brought tears to his eyes. He breathed in deeply through his nose, half expecting that same scent now but catching, instead, a distinct whiff of something rotten.

God! Can't they at least keep the cars clean?

He opened his eyes and stared angrily at the back of the driver's neck, but noticing there, for the first time, more scars to match those on his hands, continued to say nothing.

The galling thing was that, up until the drive home that night a year ago, it had been a brilliant week for him: a big promotion at work, the new car as a result of the promotion, the final papers on his divorce coming through. He had felt a huge sense of freedom. No wonder he had celebrated with a drink or two. No wonder he had wanted to drive fast, and feel powerful and abandoned and alive.

And it would have been fine if it hadn't been for the snow. The snow making it so hard to see. And there *must* have been ice on the road. Must have been.

And the other car . . .

As they turned a corner, a car passed them going the opposite way, its headlights raking through the interior of the taxi, glaring into his eyes and stretching shadows over the driver. It shook him back into the present. He glanced out of his window and couldn't recognize where they were. He would have expected that they would have joined the main road by now, then they would go up onto the ring road, bypass the town center, and on to the venue. But maybe there was a problem on one of the roads that way and the GPS was automatically diverting them. Or, on the other hand, maybe his driver was trying to prolong the journey to push the fare up. Well, if that was the case, then he'd picked the wrong man. He took out his phone again and clicked on its GPS. A map filled the screen, a pointer tracing the car's progress as they went. They were certainly a little off course, but only a little. Not enough that he could be sure of deliberate deceit. Not yet, at least.

But I'm watching you now, sonny boy. You just try it and I'll know. I'll get you sacked at the very least.

He wasn't above using his influence to do damage to other people's lives. There had been that keen young policeman after the accident, for instance.

"I just wondered," the cop had said, in his tremulous

voice, "if you had seen anything. Only, Mr. Korbin went missing the same day as your accident. And from what we know, he must certainly have been driving somewhere nearby, and at around the same time."

No, he had said, he hadn't seen anything, which was almost true as his eyes had been closed for the crucial seconds when he had drifted onto the wrong side of the road. But he hadn't fallen asleep. Not for more than an instant anyway, and you couldn't blame him for that.

Nor had he lied when he had said that he did not recognize the photograph of poor missing Mr. Korbin. He hadn't properly seen the driver of the other car in the split second available to him. And then it had swerved violently to avoid him and careered off the road and into the woodland. Once he had reined his own car back under control, he had braced himself for the inevitable sound of the other car crashing, somewhere in the woods, but it never came. And he did not go back to look, or even check his mirror. And by the time he had his own crash (there *must* have been ice), he was another mile down the road.

"At the next intersection, turn right."

Oh no. That did it. They were definitely going in the wrong direction now. They weren't heading for the conference center at all.

"Hey!"

The driver made no sign of having heard him.

"Hey! I don't know how stupid you must think I

am, matey boy, but you're not going to get away with this kind of thing with me."

Still there was no response. Just the sound of the engine, the sound of the road, and the rhythm of the wipers clearing not rain now, but snow from the windshield.

"I booked you to take me to the Hardwicke Center, not for a scenic drive through—"

He realized for the first time exactly where they were now.

"Through the woods."

He was back there. Where it had all happened. Precisely one year ago.

What was this?

They had never found the other car. Never found Mr. Korbin. He had assumed they would, and feared that they would connect the two accidents. He had feared the inconvenience, embarrassment, and expense of a court case against him. But the snow must have covered Korbin's tracks. A week or so later, when it at last thawed away, he had worried that something must surely turn up, but he had known better than to go back to look. He'd heard nothing on the news. There had been that one visit from the eager young policeman, but a quiet word with the chief constable the next time they played golf together had ensured he wasn't troubled again.

It made no sense that the crashed car had never been discovered but, as time went by, he'd found he wondered about it less and less. Some miracle had saved him and he had chosen not to question how.

The snow was heavier now but the driver took no notice. If anything, they were accelerating.

"Stop this!"

He remembered now the photograph the constable had shown him. It wasn't only of Mr. Korbin. It was a family photograph: dark and stocky Mr. Korbin, his pretty young wife, his grinning son. Korbin had one burly arm around his wife's thin waist, his other bent at his side, his hand resting on his son's shoulder.

"I said, stop this! Stop the car!"

The driver said nothing but took one hand from the steering wheel and moved it to the stick shift.

The photograph must have been taken on a sunny day. The Korbins were all squinting in the sunlight. Mrs. Korbin wore a light cotton floral-print dress, the boy wore shorts and a T-shirt, and Mr. Korbin had rolled up the sleeves of his collared shirt. On his left forearm there was a tattoo: writing, though it was impossible to tell exactly what it said.

It was clear enough on the burly forearm of the driver now, though, as he shifted up a gear and accelerated once more.

The tattoo said: *Scream if you want to go faster!*

"Please," he shouted. "Please don't—"

And then he was blinded by bright light. A red BMW was coming at them far too quickly and on the wrong side of the road. He was thrown against the door as the taxi swerved violently. He felt the bump and lurch of it leaving the road, but they did not slow down. He was pressed back into his seat as the car sped over a short patch of rough earth and on into the woodland.

"Oh God!"

Something was happening to the driver's skin. The scratches and scars on his hands and neck were opening up to weep tears of blood.

The car swerved through the trees, branches crashing against the roof and windshield.

The driver's hands were clamped tight on the steering wheel, his body hunched in concentration as he steered them, at terrifying speed, deeper into the woods. Lines of blood were extending back from his growing scars.

When, at last, the driver turned his head, he recognized Korbin's face at once, even through its mask of blood.

The woods were denser now. They were racing straight toward a sturdy and immovable tree trunk. There was no way around it, and they were traveling absurdly fast.

He threw his arms pointlessly up in front of his face, but through the gap between them he could still see the tree trunk growing in an instant to fill the full extent of the headlights' glow, and the driver's face bloodied, decayed, and distorted, grinning back at him in the instant before his annihilation.

Time stopped. The snowflakes hung in the air. He could see the pattern of the bark on the tree, a trailing thread from his coat sleeve catching the light from the dashboard, the unholy leering smile of the driver.

There was a scream forming in his lungs and it would never be released.

"You have reached your final destination."

*M*r. Harlow's head is slightly bowed over his note-pad, and he remains hunched and still for a moment. Then he taps a finger lightly, once, on the open page, as if placing a final full stop, and closes the pad. Only then does he half raise his eyes to look for a reaction. The others gently nod their approval.

"Thank you," says the pale man, with a slow, small bow of the head.

Jack closes his eyes and shakes his head, as he tries to dislodge from it the images that the story has put there: not only those that the story described, but also the ones that Jack has imagined for the moments after the end. He doesn't want them in there.

"Thank you, Mr. Osterley," says Mr. Harlow quietly. Then, after a pause, he draws in a modest breath and blows out his candle. He allows himself a weak smile as he pushes his chair back from the table, away from the light, and leans back, happy to retire into darkness.

"Yes. Thank you, Mr. Harlow," says Piotr the giant. His impressively bushy beard quivers with glee as he speaks in a heavy accent that Jack can't quite place. "Is very good tale! Is magnificent. It give me the geese bump, is so scary! And I am bravest man from my village. I do not scare so easy! Oh no! Not on my nelly!"

"Thank you, Piotr," says Mr. Osterley calmly and quietly. "Your enthusiasm has been noted." There seems to be no reproach in his voice, but still the big man falls instantly silent, like an over-excited schoolboy who's been told off.

"I just like story," he mumbles, hunched over now, as if trying to compress his immense frame into a smaller shape.

"Oooh, and quite right, too," says a woman's voice. Jack looks over. She is quite small, this woman, and enormously untidy. Everything about her is untidy: her clothes, her hair, even her skin somehow seems to be the wrong size for her. She looks like a baby bird with scruffy explosions of tangled hair that set off in a variety of directions from her head, like patches of newly sprouting feathers. "It was a smashing story. Well done, Mr. H," she says. Her head jerks as she speaks, her eyes swiveling madly to maintain a fix on whoever she's looking at. She reminds Jack of his great-aunt Millie. She might easily be just as mad, too. The association makes Jack feel a tiny bit more at home, just a little more at ease. She gives a strange little laugh. "Ooh, yes, just smashing."

"Perhaps," says Mr. Osterley, "we might have your contribution next, Mrs. Trent."

"Ooh, now, dear, you really must call me Josephine. I can't be doing with formality, me. I've no time for it."

Mr. Osterley's lips purse, just the tiniest amount, and he pauses before he speaks again. "Josephine, then. If you would be so kind."

"Of course, my dear. Of course. Now then, tonight I

thought I'd tell you a story that happened in my own village. Imagine! Ooh, it were quite a to-do at the time, I can tell you. Do you like cats?" Grinning and twitching, her head angled up one way, her eyes turned to look in another direction completely, it's impossible to tell if she's asking anyone in particular, but in any case, she doesn't pause for a reply. "Some people go all soppy for them, don't they? Never understood it myself. I quite like a dog, you know, if it's the right kind of dog. Nothing too small and yappy. But cats I don't really have time for, myself, and—"

"If you would be so kind, Josephine, please . . ." says the pale man. There is only a tiny grain of exasperation in his tone, but it works well enough. Josephine's jolting head comes to a standstill and her eyes rest briefly on Mr. Osterley's still, expressionless face.

"Of course," she says, and balls her bony hands up into tight fists. "Get on with it, Josephine. Well, then. Here we go."

Oswald

Well, it was a funny old business from the start. From before the start, even. But I'll start at the beginning anyway. I can always go back, now, can't I? Oh, but then, when *was* the beginning? Well, there's a question and no mistake. But I tell you what I'll do: I'll start with Helena. I'll start with Helena dying.

So, Helena died. Well, you knew that already, I just said.

Oh, anyway, Helena died, but nobody was surprised, because she was very old and she'd been ill almost forever, and nobody cared very much because, well, let's be honest: she was a horrible, *horrible* woman. *Nobody* liked her. Even the other people in the village that nobody liked: they didn't like her, either.

And Helena, so far as anyone could tell, didn't like anybody. She'd been a difficult and lonely child, and over the years she'd grown into a difficult and lonely old woman. A difficult, lonely, bitter, spiteful, poisonous old woman. She lived in a big old house away from the main village and she'd go days without seeing anyone at all, which suited her. And, to be fair, it suited everyone else, too. Well, you can imagine.

So she was lonely, by choice, but she did have her

cats. She'd had a fair few of them over the years, but by the time I'm talking about, at the end, she had three: Tabitha, Tiptree, and Oswald. And when she was very ill, with only months to live, so the doctor told her, and she couldn't really cope anymore, her nephew came to stay to help her out. He shopped and he cooked and he cleaned and he looked after the cats.

He was a sweet boy, Roland, just lovely. And *so* loyal to his aunt. She treated him just as badly as she treated every other human being she ever met— shouting at him and calling him stupid and never a word of thanks for all he did—but he wouldn't say a word against her.

He wouldn't even speak ill of those cats, and they were right little demons, let me tell you. Tabitha and Tiptree were bad enough, but Oswald, oh dear, Oswald was an unholy *terror*. Times I saw poor Roland with scratches on his arms and face, and he'd tell me some tale about tackling the brambles in Aunt Helena's garden, but I could see: those scratches weren't from any brambles.

Now, like I say, old Dr. Whitfield had said Helena had only a short while left to live. Two or three months, if she was lucky, he said. Well, Helena was as bloody-minded and stubborn about that as she was about everything else, and she didn't die after three months and she didn't die after four, or six, or even a year . . . In fact, Dr. Whitfield himself died before Helena did. Went to bed one night telling Mrs. Whitfield he had terrible indigestion and it turned out he was having a heart attack. It might not have been fatal if Mrs. W had been upstairs with him to get help, but she was downstairs in a huff because he'd blamed her dumplings. Silly man. Still, if he *had* lived, then it wouldn't have done much for his reputation, would it? People knowing that he couldn't even diagnose his own heart attack!

Anyway, Helena lived on for three years and a little bit more before she finally passed on, and she didn't get any kinder in her last days. That poor boy Roland took all manner of abuse from her, and it wore him down, you could see. Oh, he'd been a lovely lad when he arrived. He was a fine boy: bright and cheerful and kind. Couldn't do enough for you. And he was still trying his best at the end, but you could see that some of the old woman's poison had seeped in. He'd be just a little bit short with you, and he always looked so tired, the poor boy. He looked, well . . . he looked broken.

But even then, when Helena did finally die, he was proper upset about it. I wouldn't have blamed him if he'd had a party. I would have. There would have been plenty who'd've been happy to celebrate the occasion. But there was a decent turnout at the funeral, for all that. More for Roland's sake than out of respect for the departed, mind, and old Mrs. Collins just along for a good feed at the wake as usual. Couldn't resist a ham roll, that one. It was a sunny day for the burial, and you couldn't help feeling like it was a rather jolly occasion. Not really funereal at all. I swear the vicar was absolutely *beaming* at times, you know, when he thought nobody was looking.

A few days later and they had the reading of the will. And the thing was, with no friends and no other relatives (her rich husband had died *years* before, and who could blame him), Helena had left Roland *everything*. Now, there was a *bit* of money—not a fortune, but a tidy enough amount—but the main thing was that he got the house.

Only there was a catch. There was a condition in the will that Roland couldn't *sell* the house, or at least not yet. He had to live in it and carry on looking after the cats, and only after they'd all died could he sell it.

Well, you can imagine, he wasn't especially keen to stay. He'd not exactly had a whale of a time in that house and he certainly wasn't fond of those blessed animals. But the house was in a right old state from generations of cats roaming around the place scratching and chewing and doing their business wherever they pleased, so what Roland decided was that he'd stay living there while he got the place tidied up a bit, then, by the time the cats had all passed on and he was able to sell, it'd be looking at its best.

So now we see a bit more of Roland around the village for a while, and he seems a bit happier now, with his aunt gone, but it doesn't last long. You see, as dreadful as Helena was to everybody, she always spoiled those cats, and Oswald in particular. But now Roland's in charge and he isn't treating them like royalty, like they're used to, so they act up proper terrible-like. Roland's trying to make repairs around the house and they're tearing around the place, or they're fighting amongst themselves. And they're bringing in dead mice and whatever and getting blood and fur all over the carpets in rooms that Roland's just got clean. So you'd forgive him—anyone would—if he was completely sick of those bloody animals (pardon my French) by now. You wouldn't blame him a bit if he wished they all just died as soon as you like and he could have a bit of peace and quiet and sell the house and go. Off to somewhere nice with no cats. But he still doesn't complain. Well, hardly at all. And he's still blaming the bramble patch for all the new scratches he's got, and not a soul believes him.

And then Tabitha dies, and despite it all you can see he's proper upset about it. Apparently she got into a fight with Oswald, who chased her out onto the driveway just as Roland was backing the car out of the garage. There's no consoling him afterward. *If only I'd been paying more attention, I might have seen her. Maybe I could have stopped in time.* Well, there's no use thinking like that, is there? The cat's no less dead for worrying about it, is she? I try to cheer him up. I say, "Look on the bright side, Roland: one down, two to go," but he takes it the wrong way.

He's still brooding on it a week later when Tiptree dies, too. Just drops down dead. Old age, most likely, and you'd think there's no way Roland can blame himself this time, but bless me, he finds a way. He reckons that Tiptree died from a broken heart, grieving for Tabitha. Now, as I say, I think he's a sweet boy but, ooh, this kind of nonsense gets my goat.

So now Roland is living in that big old house with no one for company except Oswald. And Oswald is just a devil. Always has been. Nice as pie for Helena—except for that one time she tried to put a collar on him and he scratched her to blazes—but a right monster to everyone else. And he's gotten worse as he's gotten older, and worse again for losing Helena, and again and again for Tabitha and Tiptree dying. Roland can't get near him now, not that he would want to if he had any sense. Which, if you're asking me, he doesn't.

Anyway, we don't see much of Roland around the village for a while. He's right busy getting on with all the work around the house and it makes him a bit of a recluse. Then Mr. Cutler bumps into him at the ironmonger's over in Freckingham one day and says afterward that he doesn't look so good. And Mrs. Curtain spots him in his car, freshly scarred she says, over near Westerby. I wonder if he's eating properly and drop by once in a while with soup or a stew, and he takes it from me and says thank you, but he doesn't smile and he never once invites me in.

He's a hard worker, though, I'll say that for him. Works all hours on the house, he does. He does the small jobs himself and pays to get men in to do anything he can't manage: you know, plastering and plumbing and such. Of course Oswald hates all the disruption and kicks up a hell of a fuss ('scuse my language) and that slows things down a bit. Some small furry dead thing gets brought into the house in the night and ends up in the plasterwork. And the plumber, eating supper in The Crown one evening, shows us all a nasty gash on his leg and boasts about the bonus Roland paid him in compensation.

A couple of days later Roland gets hurt, too. A bloomin' great bookcase topples over when Oswald jumps from the top of it, and Roland's right underneath it when it falls. Might have killed him, easy as pie. Must have been a heck of a weight. Dangerous things, books—I won't have 'em in the house. Well, anyway, it doesn't kill Roland, but it does put him in the hospital for a few days. I think at this point that it feels pretty much like a holiday for him, lying in bed all day, everything laid on, and not a cat in sight. He's as chirpy as I've seen him in a long while when I go and visit. Then, when he gets home, he finds that Oswald has finally gone to meet his maker while he was away.

It's not been a dramatic death; it's just that the years have finally caught up with him. It was probably only spite that was keeping him going anyway, I reckon, so with nobody else about to make suffer he probably couldn't see the point anymore. Roland finds him curled up in his favorite spot: in front of the fireplace in the sitting room. He looks *so* peaceful, but it's hard for Roland to appreciate because of the stench. It turns out that in his last moments Oswald had lost all control of his bowels. All over one of Helena's best rugs, too. Worth a fortune, it is. Well, *was* worth a fortune.

Now, at this point Roland's meant to be taking things very easy for at least the next couple of days. But he's not been back five minutes and he's already out in the garden burying Oswald. It's a big hole he digs, too, because he buries him all wrapped up in the rug, which is beyond help. Mrs. Curtain drops by to see him and finds Roland standing on top of the new grave, pressing down the earth, shining with sweat. And there's no disguising his smile. He looks as if a weight has been lifted from him. He looks relieved and happy, and there's not a person in the village who would begrudge him that.

He's even seen in the pub later, getting tiddly on cider, and he's quite the happy chatterbox. It really looks like he's turned a corner.

But then a day or so later, back working on the house, there's some kind of problem with the upstairs lights: they go off sudden-like one night. So Roland calls in an electrician the next day, and he takes a look and finds a break in one of the wires.

"Looks like it's been gnawed through," this fella says. "Probably mice," he says. "You should think about getting a cat, you know," he says.

Roland says he'll buy a mousetrap. And he does. He nips over to Freckingham and picks one up at the village store. Lovely little shop, that. Beautiful pork pies. Anyway, Roland goes home, sets the trap with a lump of cheddar for bait, then goes to The Crown for his supper. Well, the cider gets the best of him again, so he's a little bit wobbly walking back up the road afterward, but he manages to remember to check the trap when he gets in, and the funny thing is: it's been sprung, but there's no mouse. And the bit of cheese is just by it, which is odd. But he thinks maybe he just didn't set it right, so he sets it again, really carefully this time, and puts it back. Then he flops down in the good armchair and, what with the cider and the walk home and everything, he soon dozes off.

He's there a good while, slumped over to one side and one arm hanging down, but perfectly content and sleeping like a baby, despite hanging off the chair all awkward-like.

It's an hour or so later when he starts to wake up. His eyes are closed, and he's still not thinking anything, but he's just faintly aware of something touching his hand. It's the lightest touch, a lovely feeling, brushing slowly across the back of his hand, just gently stroking him. Soft as silk it is. And his eyelids begin to creak open, and his mind starts to focus, and he thinks: not silk. No, not silk. Something else.

Fur.

Oh, he's awake now! Wide-awake all of a sudden, and he pulls his hand up ever so fast, like it's been scalded, and he shrieks the same way, and his eyes have snapped wide-open. He stares down at the floor and there's nothing there, of course, so he looks around the room, everywhere, all frantic-like. And, bless me, but there's nothing there at all. So he's sitting there, the one hand holding the other, telling himself he dreamed it, but his skin is tingling, and his heart is racing. And the mousetrap has sprung again.

He sits there trembling, staring at it for a while. Then he goes to his bed and he pulls the covers up and he leaves the lamp on. All night he doesn't sleep for more than ten minutes at a time, and the slightest creak or squeak around the old house wakes him up and sets him trembling.

When dawn breaks, as usual there's no bird singing to let him know. Helena used to say that Oswald had scared all the birds away years ago, but I reckon it's just as likely they were avoiding *her*.

Roland's been dozing, but he feels like he's not slept for days. His head is a right old muddle, all fuzzy and jumbled. He turns off the lamp, gets up, and goes over to the window and looks out. And, oh, it's a beautiful morning. Just lovely. The bedroom window looks out over farmland and the sunlight is lighting up the frost on the plowed fields, and the sky is clear.

He opens the window and breathes in some of that fresh morning air, and it's as delicious as a drink of cold water on a hot day. Just for a moment he stands there and, oh, he feels so calm. His whole world is still and silent, and he likes it that way.

But then it isn't silent anymore. It's only a little

noise, but it's just enough that he can't ignore it. It's coming from downstairs, a little high *plink*. Just a single note played on the piano, but it seems to ring on and on. Then, when it seems to be fading away to nothing, it sounds again.

Now, that piano hasn't been played in years. It was Helena's late husband's, but he passed away very many years ago, terribly young. ("Gone to a better place," said the vicar at the time, and you could tell he meant it more than usual.) But now there's this high, soft note coming from it, again and again. Roland can barely make it out, it's so quiet to begin with, and coming from down the stairs and around a corner, but he winces every time he hears it.

Anyway, eventually he decides he can't ignore it any longer and he sets off downstairs to investigate, but he's a bit nervous about it, so he decides to take some kind of a weapon with him. There's still books on the floor from when the bookcase went over so he picks up a really hefty one—a big old dictionary is my guess—and takes that. It's the best he can do from what's at hand. He creeps down the stairs and the piano note keeps playing over and over, annoying as a dripping tap.

Roland makes his way, quiet as anything, along the hallway to the living room door. It's open just a crack, but not enough to get a look at the piano. So he pushes the door ever so gently open. He's trying so hard to be quiet, but oiling door hinges is still on his list of things to do, so it creaks, and then, all of a sudden, there's this quick flurry of notes from the piano—*plink plonk plonk*—high to low, and a thump as the stool falls over, but by the time Roland gets in, there's nothing to see. So he stands there for a bit, and he's sort of angry and relieved and scared all at the same time.

Once he's calmed down a bit, he closes the lid over the keyboard. He wants to lock it shut but the key isn't there, so he goes off to the bedroom to look in Aunt Helena's music box. It's a little carved wooden jewelry box that plays a clockwork tune when you open the lid. Helena kept all kinds of junk in it, so he thinks maybe that's where the key will be. He finds the box and opens it up, and it's still wound up, so it plays its little tune as he rummages around inside. And in among the earrings and buttons and foreign coins and an extra-strong mint and all kinds of other things he finds the piano key. And he also finds a small black leather collar with a bell on it: the one that Helena couldn't get Oswald to wear. And now he remembers his aunt telling him about it, back when he was a little boy.

"It was the only time Oswald ever scratched me," she said. "I tried to put that collar on him because he'd been killing birds and bringing them into the house. Feathers and guts everywhere. Terrible mess. So I tried to put the collar on him so the birds would hear the bell and keep away from him, but he wouldn't have it. He hated it! He kicked and he squirmed and he fussed!

So I held him down tight and got the collar around his neck, and I was just trying to do up the buckle when he lashed out at me with his claws. Look, here, he cut the back of my hand, here, see. Do you see the scars? Gushing with blood, it was. And Oswald just jumped free and ran off. He didn't come back for three days. I was so worried. And when he did finally come back, well, I never tried to put a collar on him again. And then eventually the birds just started to stay away anyway, as if they knew."

It's the most he can remember Aunt Helena saying to him in one go, and he smiles at the memory of it, but that isn't why.

"He hated it . . ." he says.

And then he buckles the collar onto his wrist. And the next day passes without incident. And the next day, and the next.

He's in The Crown a bit more regular for a while after that, and much more chatty, too. He tells us about what's been going on and how scared he got, how he'd started to imagine all sorts of silly things and, oh, isn't it funny how ridiculous he's been? But he's fine now, he says. Just fine.

But he keeps wearing the cat collar on his wrist. He says, if you point it out, that it's just to remind him of how silly he was, *starting to believe in ghosts, for goodness' sake*! And we chuckle along with him. He's a nice lad and we're glad to see him out a bit more.

And before long he's only ever telling us all about

how the work on the house is going and not mention-
ing the cat at all. The collar's still on his wrist, mind,
but we don't mention it. And he's starting to feel
quite at home in the village now, and he's thinking
maybe he won't sell the house after all. Maybe he'll
stay. With all the work he's done he's got quite a reputation as a handyman now, and he does the odd bit of
work for folk around the village, and round about. He
thinks he can make a living at it if he works it right.
It's not as if he needs to earn much, and he can always
rent out a room or two in the house for a bit extra if
need be.

A week or two later I'm passing by the house on my
bicycle, and bless me if Roland doesn't nearly knock
me down in his car as he comes racing home. He gets
out, all flustered and fussing, and he won't stop apologizing. I tell him not to worry; I'm fine. But why was he
in such a hurry? Well, he tells me that Helena's old
lawyer is coming over with papers to finalize the trans-
fer of the house. Once Roland signs, it'll be all his. But
he'd been out doing a little repair job for someone out
in Freckingham, lost track of the time, and now the
lawyer, Mr. Buckley, is due any minute. And then he
starts apologizing all over again and I have to get quite
blunt with him to make him stop. Then I tell him
congratulations—about the house, I mean—and I
shake him by the hand and say how I hope he will stay
because he's such a fine young man and he's a proper
credit to the village.

Well, he's a bit embarrassed by this—he's rotten at accepting compliments—and he really needs to get in and clean himself up before the lawyer arrives. So he thanks me, and dashes indoors, and I cycle off on my way. But as I do, I wonder why it is that I don't feel right. My guts are churning, like I'm worried about something, but I can't think for the life of me what it could be. I'm still thinking about it when I arrive at Thornely, the next village over, where I'm picking up a dress I was having altered.

Well, it's when I open the door to the shop that I realize what's been bothering me. You see, there's a bell that rings when the door opens and that makes me realize: when I shook Roland's hand, there was no bell. He wasn't wearing the collar on his wrist. And, well, that's a relief because that's a good thing, not anything to worry about after all. I think it's just grand that he's finally seen sense and stopped wearing it, and it only makes me think of him all the more fondly.

I see the ambulance parked outside when I'm coming back the other way and, oh, it does give me a turn. My heart's in my mouth as I stop, and I see poor Roland led out the front door and helped into the back of the ambulance. He's not making any fuss, mind, but his eyes are wider than I've ever seen anyone's before, and he's muttering quietly to himself, and he looks quite, quite mad. And those wide eyes are staring out from a bloody face. And that's *not* swearing, because he is just

59

covered in blood. I almost scream. His clothes are torn and his skin is torn and he is covered in blood.

Mr. Buckley says that's how he found him. He thinks Roland did it to himself somehow, just went mad and slashed at himself with something sharp, and the police and the doctors are happy enough with that explanation, too. They certainly can't get any sense out of Roland to suggest otherwise. Mind you, they can't find anything in the house that could have made those cuts, either. I try to make a bit of a fuss about it all, but it's not as if I've got any better explanation. Not one I'm happy to say out loud anyway.

The next day I bump into Mrs. Curtain's niece. It turns out it was her that Roland had been doing the work for the day before. She'd been heading over to return Roland's bracelet, she says, the one with the funny little bell on it. She saw him take it off before he set to unblocking her drain, and then he must have forgotten to put it back on again. She'd tried to take it back to him at the house but it didn't seem like anyone was home so she'd just pushed it through his letter box.

"He's not still got one of them cats of Helena's, has he?" she says.

"No," I say.

"I didn't think so," she says. "Only when I pushed the bracelet through, and the bell jingled as it hit the floor, well, I could have sworn I heard a cat. Mind you, if it had been, then, coo, it wasn't a happy one!" And then she's off on her way, running to catch the bus.

*

I visit Roland for a while after that, at the special hospital, but he never speaks to me. Not to me, and not to any of the doctors and nurses, neither. I keep going anyway, but he won't touch the fruit I take him; it just rots in the bowl. And I talk to him. I try to tell him what's been going on in the village, but he takes no notice.

After a while they ask me not to go anymore. They say poor Roland has become quite distressed, and more and more difficult. You know, violent. He keeps scratching people. It's very upsetting. He was always such a kind and gentle boy before, and now he's just a devil.

Though apparently he does sometimes bring gifts for his nurses.

Mostly birds.

*J*osephine, having come to a halt, sits in a curious frozen pose, her neck craning, her head tilted. Her eyes are bulging and seemingly staring, fascinated, at an empty corner of the ceiling. Her hands are clasped together over her chest, tightly entangled in a messy knot of bony fingers. Her mouth is puckered tightly closed, as if it's trying to disappear altogether. She is humming very softly, and her head is nodding, just the tiniest amount, in time.

"Thank you, Josephine," says Mr. Osterley, and Josephine's head dips forward as a grateful smile stretches out across her face. She looks like a child delighted by the praise of a parent.

"Yes, thank you, Josephine," says friendly Frances. "I enjoyed that very much."

Josephine grins all the wider. Jack even thinks that she might be blushing, though it's a little hard to tell by candlelight. Some of the others offer up compliments, and Josephine shrugs and smirks in embarrassed delight. Jack mumbles something, too, but he's a little distracted. He's thinking about the rumors he's heard about this place, and just for a moment he's wondering how much of what he's heard can possibly be true.

"Is shame the kitty cats is so horrible," says Piotr, and everyone else turns their attention to him. "I have kitty cat before, and she very good. She best mouse catcher in my village. Even better than my sister. I still sometimes miss. Is sad." The exuberant forest of his beard closes up around his mouth, leaving no trace of where it was, his head settles heavily, sinking down between the sad shrug of his enormous shoulders, his eyes glisten.

"Oh, Piotr, lovey," says Josephine. "You poor lamb." There is a subtle hint of distaste in Mr. Osterley's expression now, but he keeps it out of his voice. "Thank you, Josephine," he says again, and raises the fingers of one hand in a tiny gesture directed at Josephine's candle.

"Oh yes, dear. Of course," she says. "Mustn't go prattling on now." And she leans forward and, with a sharp stab of breath, blows out her candle, then shifts her chair back, away from the table and into the gloom.

"Very good," says Mr. Osterley. "And now perhaps, Piotr, you might take your turn?"

Jack relaxes a little at this, happy not to have been chosen, and Piotr cheers up considerably, too. His gleeful grin is exhumed from his beard.

"Ha! Oh, yes, please, mister. It is pleasure. I have very good tale for you. Is story from big time ago in my country that my grandmother tell me when I was boy. You will like very much, I think. Oh yes. Is like fairy tale, only is true. My grandmother swear by her moustache that is true. So must be so."

Piotr settles himself, pulls his mighty torso upright, and sits up very straight. He scans a stern look around the table, ensuring everyone's attention. And then he begins.

63

The Red Tree

Once, in land near mine, there is woodcutter in little village. One day he go out to chop down big, mighty oak tree. He is not long from being started when skinny fellow appear, all sweaty and running fast, and he say: "Sell me horse." But wood-cutter, he need horse, of course, so he say: "No, thank you very much." But sweaty fellow, he go to horse anyway, like he is to steal it. So woodcutter hit him on head with ax. Not with sharp end of blade, only with back to make him stop, but still he kill sweaty fellow. Is big ax for cutting of big tree, is very heavy. *Oh no!* he think. Dead sweaty fellow is dressed all fine. Maybe he is important man and now woodcutter has killed and is make the big trouble.

Then king's knights appear, and woodcutter think, *Oh no, is very bad!*

But no! Dead man is bad prince from country over river. Bad prince, he was running away from king's knights. King's knights very happy bad prince dead. They take woodcutter to see king, they say he big hero. King, he give woodcutter many gifts as reward, songs are written saying how brave he is, his fame grow, and pretty girls of kingdom dream of him. Now wood-cutter, he forget all about his village, hang up his ax on

67

wall of house near palace, and he start spending his money on pleasures of city.

But near village, in far part of kingdom, there is dark forest where many young men disappear. Nobody know why. They go into forest—maybe hunting, maybe looking for mushrooms, maybe picking flowers for pretty girl, who know?—and they never come out. People there, they very unhappy, and frightened, you know? They tell all kind of tales. They say murderous beasts in forest, or they say evil spirits, but story that they tell most say there is red tree that lures men to doom. Is very bad. They scared and they don't know what to do. So when, you know, story-singing man . . . er, what is word? Minstrel! Yes, minstrel. When minstrel come to village and sing song about woodcutter's brave deeds, they think: here is man to help us, and they send message to king. And so woodcutter, he is summoned to palace.

He get there, and he wait awhile, and awhile more, and then big tall fellow who is chamberlain come and take him to king.

"Your Majesty," say woodcutter, and he kneel down. "How might I serve you?"

The king, he has forgot all why woodcutter is here, so he ask chamberlain, and then chamberlain start to explain to king. And then after little while king is bored and so he tell chamberlain to deal with wood-cutter while king go off and have nap.

"Is curse of Northern Woods," say chamberlain. "Is

problem there, and king, he like you go there and solve, yes?" And he say it like question, but is not question that woodcutter should answer. So woodcutter he stay quiet. He smart cookie, but he look not so keen on going to Northern Woods.

"You very good before, when you kill evil Prince Frederick from land of enemies," say chamberlain. "Land of enemies make war with us, we win war, we make country bigger, king make more money. Is good thing. King, he hope you like house and lands and money he give you?"

"His Majesty very generous," say woodcutter.

"Yes, indeedy," say chamberlain, and he roll his eyes. "So, king have favor to ask."

And then chamberlain explain about Northern Woods, and people who go missing, and legends about red tree, and there is, too, other legends about silver ghost, and he roll his eyes again and say: "Tch! Country folk! We would take no notice, only queen's maid's cousin live in village, and queen say we will do something. So we send you with guards, make sure you arrive all safe. Make sure no bandits in woods slow you down. Then you chop down red tree, lift curse, calm down superstitious local peoples, and everybody happy." And this time he not even pretend to make question. Woodcutter, he have no choice.

"Is my honor to serve king," he say.

"You bet your boots, mister," say chamberlain. "You leave at dawn."

69

The next day is long ride to Northern Woods. Woodcutter and escorts not waylaid by bandits on journey. Is just boring. And guards boring, too. Is enough to tell you: all very glad to arrive at village.

Tomas, son of miller, see woodcutter and guards coming and run to tell village elders, and so they come out to greet. But when they see woodcutter and guards they not so happy.

"Is that it?" say one of them. "We send to king for help and all he send is two fat old soldiers and dandy. And for this we are paying taxes?"

Guards not like being called fat and old (because they fat and old) so they say: "We not stopping. We here to deliver this fellow all safe and all sound. We go now." And they go.

Elders look at woodcutter. One of them say: "What you meant to be, anyhows?"

Woodcutter get down off horse and try to stand all brave and manly and impressive.

"I am woodcutter Yan Haval," he say, "hero of Southern Woods, slayer of evil Prince Frederick from lands to north, savior of kingdom, and proud servant of King Emil the Wise!"

"*You* are Yan Haval?" say elder. "You shorter than ballads say. Oh well. You bring ax?"

"Yes," say woodcutter, and he sigh. "I bring ax."

"I suppose you will do. Come have soup and we talk."

So they take him to house, give him soup and bread

and they tell him legend of silver ghost and red tree. Only they argue and can't agree how story go. There is red tree and there is silver ghost, and some children and menfolk go missing in woods, and some cattle and some plants die. This much they all agree. But rest? Oh boy! One say silver ghost live in red tree. One say, no, you fool, red tree grow fruit to protect from silver ghost. Another one say, you both wrong, silver ghost guard red tree. This all go on very long time and wood-cutter very bored. Also, soup is no good.

Woodcutter say, "You want me cut down red tree?" and his forehead go all wrinkles like plowed field. The elders, they have little chat between them, all quiet and whispers and secrets. Then they say to him: "Yes, please, thank you very much."

So they draw him map. Is pretty bad map, because of arguing, but give some idea of where is red tree, and woodcutter wanting to leave, so he pick up ax and walk off toward dark woods. As he go, he pass children singing in street, teasing younger boy. They sing:

"Child, don't stray in dark, dark wood,
For whether you bad or whether you good,
Where the red tree grow
From the bones below
The silver ghost will drink your blood."

Is such nonsense, think woodcutter to himself. Such silly superstitions! I find this red tree, I chop it down, I back to city in time for market day. And he smile to himself at thought of chamberlain's daughter, who he promise to take around market. She very pretty girl with hair all shiny shiny and skin like moon on water. So he stride through woods, following way marked on terrible map, and he look for red tree.

Now, is funny thing: see, he know full well all village folk just silly billies with their fears and superstitions, but as light fade and shadows grow long and dark, woodcutter, he start to find woods all scary and sinister. He feel like when he was little boy. And he realize he see and hear no birds and no animals, all he hear is own footsteps, fern and bracken under feet, sometimes crunch of twig that make heart thump harder in chest. And it get darker and all little shadows join up into one big shadow, like monster made of night that loom over him.

Now, woodcutter, he is used to forests and woods, but even so, he find he feel afraid, just a little bit. Is very annoying and he tell himself off. Silly man! And he set down his pack and he make camp for night. And he make nice fire—to keep warm, not because he is afraid of dark, oh, no. And when he sleep and he keep waking up, is because ground is hard and uncomfortable, not because sound of wind through high branches make him anxious, and not because of dreams of pale figure, glowing all silver, walking toward him with arms all outstretched.

Woodcutter wake at dawn. Fire is out, and he cold

and tired, and he not think in straight lines, and dreams he had still in head little bit, like morning mist not cleared, like echoes. But then he start to see right, and head start to clear, and echoing sounds from dream are still there. Is real sound, not dream. And is close.

Something coming.

He really scared like little boy now, so he do what little boy do and he think: *I climb tree and hide.* When he little boy he hide from village children up tree. Most people is never looking up. Is good hiding place. So he grab pack and he look all quick for good tree, and he very lucky man because straight ahead is very good tree. Bark is pale and stand out in twilight, like is saying: "Pick me! Pick me!" And has low branches make easy to climb.

He race up quick (is like up ladder is so easy) and he find comfy branch, is maybe twenty feet up, and he settle. And he stay very still and he look down through branches and he look for whatever is making noise. Is rustling leaves and cracking twigs, and is louder, so must be closer now, but still he cannot see what. He shift body, just very little bit, and all slow and quiet, looking down all different angles, through all different gaps in crisscross branches. Dawn light is all broken up and branches all shiny frosty, they go all wobbly wibbly for his eyes, make head dizzy. He blink all tight and shake head and he look again, and he hear his own breathing, like sound of sawing, and see breath all clouds in cold morning air.

And he wait and he watch, and noise still is louder, but still he see nothing. And still, and still . . . Then—at last!—he glimpse some moving thing in down below. Not silver ghost, though. Is something dark. What is? He remember chamberlain talk of bandits in woods. Is man maybe? He see again something, just for little moment, and he hear all snuffling and grunts. Is no man. Then it move to where he see good through big gap in branches, and he see is boar! Is big fat boar! And boar is very not ghost! Woodcutter, he laugh, all relieved. Very short laugh like stab or punch. "Ha!" Like that. He feel like fool. He laugh again, loud, with head back and mouth all open wide.

This when he see. Through tangly branches above is something glinting all sparkles near top of tree. He decide to climb and see. Is easy at first, like before, like tree is helping. Always is place for foot to go, always is branch for hand to grip. So he climb up very fast, and he keep seeing glinting shining metal above but only little bit, and always not clear what is.

But then is tricky bit. Is place where big branch has broken off. Is only jagged sharp stump that stick out from trunk, then next branch up is long way and hard to reach. He take off pack, and jam into forked branch at feet, then he jump up. Is brave thing. Is very high up now and if he fall, is killing him. He grab branch above with both hands, but one slip off, and he swing and he nearly fall. Leg bash into sharp stump of broken branch and he cry out painful. But he hang on, and he grab on with other hand and pull up himself. He look at leg. Is cut all bloody, but not so bad.

He look up again. Flashy metal shining is easier to see now, but still not see what is. And now, also above, he see dark shapes in branches, maybe like nests or some other something like? But big nests. He climb some more. His leg hurt little bit and he go slower and have to concentrate quite hard, but he go up and up okay, and eventually he reach the shiny metal thing and is medallion. Is pretty thing. Maybe is good gift for chamberlain's daughter. He wonder how is getting there up tree. Maybe bird carry it up and it fall from nest. He look up now at nests.

Is not nests.

Is raggedy cloth, all torn up and tangled, rags swaying in breeze. And in rags is bones. Is human bones. Woodcutter, he see rib cage first, then other thing else. Maybe arm, maybe leg. And is more nests than one. Is five or six, all same, all rags and bone bodies. He make no cry, but his breath go all fast and loud, and his heart same. He think he is far enough high up tree now. He think now he go down.

But he look down and see no way. Branches is all wrong now. He try to see way he come up, but is not what he remember. Is very strange. He trying to reach leg down one way and he scrape cut against knot on trunk and, oh, it hurt very much! He howl all loud, then he try to pull leg back up, but somehow is stuck. Foot is caught between two branches somehow, and pain is hot and wet. He reach down left hand to feel, bring back up to face. Fingers dripping very red. Is bad cut. And foot still stuck.

He reach up high and take hold of branch above head, ready to pull leg free with strong pull. With bloody hand he grip branch tight and he see blood drip onto bark, run into grooves in bark. Blood is drawing red lines on branch and he is watching.

And blood disappear.

Is like blood evaporate. Or is like blood is sucked into pale bark. Is very scary strange, even to brave woodcutter. And seeing is making woodcutter all stiff and still, and he is feel like leg is stuck more tight now. He try to pull up, but only more pain. Is not moving. If only he have ax! But is below with pack. He tell himself when back down to ground, he is making revenge and chopping tree down. Is good practice before he chop also down red tree. And he smile one second.

Then he scream.

Is new pain now in right hand. He twist his head and look up and he see impossible thing. Is new twigs grown from branch this second. Is like fingers grasping hand. Is crushing hand. He try to pull it free but is no good. Twigs go more thick and more tight and hand is gripped very, very strong. So now is one leg and one hand trapped and is much pain. Woodcutter pull and twist and kick, wild and all panic, but is no good. More twigs grow, and they go thicker and they grip free hand and leg and they pull them and make still.

So now woodcutter all still all over. He cannot move one thing except to twist his head a little. And he call out to empty forest for help. He cry and scream. But only for just little while, because is new branch growing, wrapping around chest like is big snake, and it go tight, and more tight, and is squeezing air out of lungs. Is crushing big strong hero, Yan Haval, like is eggshell.

Breath of woodcutter is just tiny thing now. In, out, just little bit. Is little gasps. All he do now is watch and feel. Even to cry out, now he cannot do. And he feel chest all very so tight, and all pains is everywhere.

Very slow and all agony he twist neck and look up, up into highest branches, all frosted in cold morning air. And he see branches is all icy silver. Is silver like ghost.

And all slow, tree is growing new twigs. Is like teeth of wood, like teeth of snake, like wooden *fangs* all biting in his flesh, growing into him. Is so much pain. Is no words for this pain.

And woodcutter feel blood is all spilling out, running down his body, running down onto tree. And he strain his head to look down, to see his blood. Staining clothes all torn and ragged, and dripping down all fast. Is like red stream flowing down grooves of bark. Is painting bark.

Is making red tree.

*J*ack sits bolt upright, his arms stretched down by his sides, his hands clutching at the seat of his chair. His chest feels tight, as if he is himself caught in the crushing branches of the red tree, and his breathing is rapid and shallow. He fixes his eyes on the table in front of him. He doesn't want to look at anyone else just at the moment, not until he's calmed down. He looks at the pattern of the grain in the wood.

Then, when this makes him think of the tree, he moves his attention to his candle, sees the molten wax dripping down the sides, like the woodcutter's blood. So he stares very hard at the candle holder. It is a dull bronze dome with a hole in the top and it doesn't remind him of anything. It is the plainest, most boring thing, and he studies it closely until he is breathing more or less normally again.

Piotr, his enormous hands gripping the edge of the table, is leaning forward and swinging his head from side to side, surveying the others, gazing at them with wide puppyish eyes, looking for their reaction. Weather-beaten Mr. Fowler is the first to respond.

"Well, that's a grand tale, sir, and well told. I've heard few finer, and you know I have heard very many in my time. Thank you."

"So glad you like," says Piotr, and continues to swing his nodding head from side to side in a grateful arc, taking in the smiling approval of all but one of the

*others around the table. He doesn't notice the exception
at first, but Jack does.*

*Next to Frances Crane is a woman in her fifties,
with cruel eyes and a hooked nose. She makes a tiny
snorting noise, and Jack looks over at her, but without
moving his head: just darts his eyes in her direction. She
has a rather sour expression on her face. Jack imagines
it must be one she finds a lot of use for.*

*Piotr frowns massively, his face a caricature of disap-
pointment. "You do not like, Mrs. Professor?" he says.*

*"Oh, it's a jolly enough little tale of its kind, I
suppose," says the professor. "But it's not really what
we're here for, is it? More of a folktale, really. Folktales
from Eastern Europe were something of a specialty
of mine back at the university, you see, so I do know
about these things. Your little story seems to be nothing
more than a slight variation on an old Polish tale, with
a few elements of one of the Mother Adela stories
from Romania thrown in for flavor. This sort of cross-
fertilization is fairly common in—"*

*"Is not Polish story," says Piotr quietly and slowly.
"Is not Romanian story." He is staring Professor Cleary
straight in the eye. "Is my grandmother's story. Is true
story my grandmother tell."*

*He stands up, and he's even bigger than Jack
thought. He leans forward, palms flat on the table,
arms braced, looming over the professor. She looks a
lot less sure of herself now.*

"She tell with little true words. Not your long fancy-pants words, Mrs. Professor Fancy-Pants." His voice is still quiet.

Professor Cleary blinks. "No. Quite." She blinks again. "And, ah . . . that very simplicity is what gives the tale its charm." She forces an amateur smile. "Very well done, Piotr. Thank you."

"Yes, thank you, Piotr. Your grandmother would be proud, I'm sure," says gray-haired Frances, smiling warmly and tapping the fingers of one hand lightly against the palm of the other in polite applause. The bangles around her wrists make more noise than her clapping. The others murmur and smile their praise, too.

Piotr's beard splits open again to unleash a wide, unruly grin, full of childish delight and bad teeth.

"Thank you, Piotr," says pale Mr. Osterley.

Piotr blows out his candle, then lifts his chair back and away from the table and sits back down on it.

"And now, perhaps, Professor Cleary, you might take your own turn?" says Mr. Osterley.

"Er, yes. Yes, of course. I, um . . ." The professor gives a little cough. She leans stiffly forward, her bony arms knotted tightly across her chest, and she looks at her candle for a moment rather than facing anyone. Then she blinks and turns her head, slowly unwraps her arms as if she's trying to conceal the fact that they were folded in the first place, and subtly shifts her expression, pulling a grimace into a false smile.

She starts to speak, in a voice made of dust.

"Well, you may think my story rather dreary and down-to-earth compared to Piotr's, I'm afraid, but I hope you'll still find it agreeable. It concerns a fellow of my former university, albeit many years before my time there . . ."

Tick, Tick, Tick . . .

P rofessor Seabright could not sleep. He could not sleep and he did not know why, and this annoyed him.

He was certainly tired. It had been a long day, and he had walked a good deal in the hot sun. Past experience suggested that exercise, sun, and plenty of sea air during the day would usually ensure a very good night's sleep to follow. But not tonight, it seemed.

He thought back to try to find some cause. Well, there had been that funny turn he'd had at lunchtime, but that had been quickly over, and he hadn't thought of it since. He had eaten nothing unusual at dinner and drunk no more nor less wine with it than usual, and he had come up to his room and to bed at the usual kind of hour. So he had expected to fall asleep at the usual time, too. He had changed into his nightwear and stacked his neatly folded clothes on a chair. The mattress had creaked a quiet hello to the weight of him as he lay upon it, and the cold bedclothes had warmed their welcome. He had lain there in serene comfort and warmth and turned off the lamp and closed his eyes.

But he could not sleep.

Something was keeping him awake. Something, like a gently prodding finger, *tap*, *tap*, *tapping* inside his head. It was only the faintest noise, but in a steady rhythm, insistently repeating. He lay there a long while, semiconscious, still hazily confident that he could ignore it and soon drift off. But once half an hour had passed, he finally admitted to himself that sleep was beyond him, and his senses roused themselves to try to identify the problem.

The blurry sound came into focus. It was barely audible, and so it was difficult to identify. But in the quiet of the night it stood out just clearly enough, and eventually he made himself sure: it was the ticking of a clock.

How odd, he thought. He had not noticed a clock when he had checked into the room in the morning, and he had stayed in the same guesthouse countless times before and there had never been a clock in any of the rooms. They were all rather similar, so he could not be absolutely sure, but he thought he had even stayed in this very room on at least one previous occasion.

Oh well. Perhaps it was a new addition. Or it had been here all along and he simply hadn't noticed it. It was close to silent, after all, so it was a wonder that he had noticed it now. But now that he had, he found himself unable to ignore it. He turned his bedside lamp back on and scanned around the room. He could not see a clock anywhere.

No matter. Now that he was awake, he might as well do something useful. He decided to take the opportunity to write up his notes.

The dean of his university had an absurd idea that the professor had been working too hard and had insisted that he take some time off. So Professor Seabright was meant to be on holiday. And he was, mostly. But while he was here he had taken the opportunity to visit the church in a nearby village. He was preparing a book on the subject of carvings and statuary in church architecture, and there were some fine gargoyles to be found at St. Radegund's that he had spent much of the day studying and sketching.

It had been a most productive and fascinating visit, albeit not wholly straightforward. The long walk there and the unseasonally hot sun had combined to make him rather weary by lunchtime, so when he'd reached the village pub on the way to the church, it had seemed like a good idea to stop in for refreshment, shade, and rest.

It had been a sound enough idea in itself, but his choice of drink had proved unwise. The landlord had suggested Devil's Wallop, an ale that he brewed himself, and the professor had politely accepted his recommendation. It had turned out to be a well-named brew of unusual darkness and strength, and the professor now found the interpretation of the notes and drawings made in the afternoon altogether a trickier task than transcribing his work from the morning.

But still, it was a challenge he relished, and sitting up in the creaking bed he read and wrote and redrew very happily for two solid hours. He took particular delight in a drawing of one especially gruesome carving that he had seen, taking care to capture its hideous features exactly.

Yawning once more, he set down his books on the bedside table, placed his spectacles on top, lay down, and turned off the lamp. He smiled when he heard the ticking of the clock again. Absorbed in his work he had entirely forgotten about it, but now, with an empty head and in dark silence, he registered again the faint beat of the seconds passing. Sleep would come soon enough, though, he felt sure.

He was wrong. A quarter hour passed, and then a quarter hour more, and he found himself still wide-awake. There was, he felt, no good reason for this, and he was not fond of things that happened without good reason.

The professor was an orderly man of fixed habits, and had never before had trouble sleeping. What is more, he had a busy day planned tomorrow that he would struggle to cope with without first getting his usual seven and a quarter hours' repose. And yet here he was in the dead of night, frustrated, as if sleeping was a skill that he had lost. As if he had simply forgotten how.

And now that quiet ticking of the unseen clock seemed not so quiet. It seemed ridiculous to blame that one small noise for his sleeplessness, but he was a logical man and he could find no other cause. Therefore, he lifted his pillow, lay his head down upon the cool sheet beneath, and then clamped the pillow firmly over his upturned ear. How it was that the ticking remained, even then, clearly audible, he was at a loss to explain, but there it was: constant, insistent, nagging. This was ridiculous. Professor Seabright's fingers clawed at the pillow, and an angry tension took hold of his whole body.

With a rather embarrassing yelping cry, the professor hurled the pillow away (though not very far; it was a feeble throw). Again, he turned the lamp on. He decided he must find the clock and stop it, or else remove it from the room. But locating it proved no simple task. No matter which way he turned, and no matter whereabouts in the room he stood, the ticking sound grew no louder nor fainter. This defied reason. And not only did his ears provide no useful clue to finding the mysterious clock, but his eyes could find no sight of it, either. Clearly, then, it must be hidden from view. Well then, he would search until he found it.

He began, as anyone who knew him even slightly would expect, in a methodical manner. Starting in one corner and working along each of the walls in turn, he opened drawers and cupboards, scrutinized the contents of shelves inch by inch, looked even in the most unlikely locations. He went so far at one point as to move the lamp over to the fireplace and look up the chimney. Then, when he was back where he had begun, he looked under the bed. He looked *in* the bed. He opened up his own luggage and meticulously checked inside (though the contents of his bags and case were known to him to the last tiny item and, he knew full well, included no timepiece). And when, having searched everywhere, he had still found nothing, he stood in the middle of the room and, with silent annoyance, noted how each quiet tick of the clock fell exactly between his short, fast, angry breaths.

This was wrong. Professor Seabright checked over every possibility in his mind, scanned once, twice around the room, looking for some possible hiding place that he had not yet considered. Nothing. There was nothing he had missed; he was sure of it. There would be no point at all in looking again. It would be a waste of time and an insult to reason.

He returned to his bed. He told himself he would sleep now. As a matter of principle he would sleep now. He would *not* allow himself to be kept awake by this nonsense. But he didn't lie down, and he did not turn off the lamp. Nor did he close his eyes, or iron out the creases in his forehead. Trembling tension filled him. Professor Seabright was not, in the normal course of events, an emotional man, but if anyone had been able to see him now, they would probably have described him as seething.

Tick, tick, tick . . .

The professor looked down at his right hand, clamped tightly around the upper part of his left arm and found that the index finger of that hand was, quite

90

without any conscious intention on his part, tapping against the sleeve of his nightshirt. Tapping in time with that infernal, unseen clock!

Tick, tick, tick . . . Tap, tap, tap . . . Tick, tick—

Now sometimes, when a man appears to have lived a calm life, ruled by reason, steady and measured and controlled, his placid exterior can actually conceal something quite different. Sometimes such a man holds within himself a bubbling well of madness and fury that, quite unseen, builds in pressure within him, awaiting its release. All it needs is a crack in that calm façade to allow the inevitable explosive outcome.

Twenty minutes later, standing with his back against the door, Professor Seabright surveyed the devastation strewn across the floor. Luckily, room eleven, like all the rooms at the guesthouse, was quite sparsely furnished. There had been only one chair for the professor to fling angrily aside as he stamped toward the bookcase. The bookcase itself contained only a very few books (and none of any interest or value) for him to scatter across the floor. The few ornaments upon the mantelpiece had been cheap but surprisingly robust, all surviving the fall as they were swept onto the floor (and the sole piece of delicate chinaware had quite by chance landed unharmed upon the bed). Nevertheless, these few items combined with the contents of the professor's luggage, the assorted fire irons, the shredded remains of the morning's newspaper, and sundry other items from around the room, had still created a considerable amount of mess when flung wildly about in frustrated rage.

It was fortunate, though, that just as he had been deciding whether or not to tip over the writing desk, Professor Seabright had been interrupted by a knock at the door.

The owner and manager of the guesthouse, Mr. Boulting, had not seemed particularly convinced by the professor's story about tripping over in the night and stumbling into the chair, but, tired as he was, he had been willing to pretend that this adequately explained all the noise. He made no mention of the screaming, and made no attempt to be let into the room to investigate further. He had always considered the professor eccentric, and he was suspicious of academics in general, but he guessed that whatever had just happened would not happen again and, if the damage was as bad as it had sounded, then the professor would pay suitable compensation without argument. Returning to his soft, warm bed seemed, in the circumstances, a much more welcoming prospect than attempting to uncover the truth of the matter. He shot the professor a dark look, tersely wished him a good night, and returned to his room.

Professor Seabright's legs folded beneath him, his back slid down the door, and he crumpled into a tangled knot on the floor. He had managed to conjure a reasonable impression of normality while talking to Mr. Boulting, but it had been an effort. He made no such effort now that he was alone again. It felt as if he was losing the one thing most dear to him: his mind.

The wild fury and abandon with which he had inflicted his clumsy violence on the contents of his room were unrecognizable to him now. It was as if they had been the actions of someone else entirely. He felt as if surely he had merely dreamed them. Or that he was still dreaming them. Yet the mess upon the floor offered clear evidence to the contrary. In amongst the debris he spotted some shards of white crockery: the remains of a fine china teacup. He felt himself to be just as broken. He sat upon the floor and shook. Tears came to his eyes and, as quietly as he could, he sobbed.

The clock was still ticking, of course, insolently counting out the seconds, each stroke thumping in the professor's head. And now two other rhythms joined it. He had cut his left hand on one of the shards of the smashed teacup and, as he hugged his knees to his chest, drops of blood fell to the floor, just as tears dripped onto the fabric of his nightshirt where it was stretched between his knees. The different rhythms of the three sounds fell in and out of time with one another, mesmerizing Professor Seabright as he stared into the chaos of scattered debris on the floor.

He picked up one of his notebooks, fallen open at the drawing of the gargoyle on which he had labored with such care earlier. The stone demon returned his stare and the professor was reminded of his earlier visit to the church.

Somewhat tired from the morning's long walk in the hot sun, and further befuddled by the effects of potent ale, the professor had been foolish to accept the vicar's eager invitation to climb the stairs to the clock tower.

The tight spiraling staircase had added dizziness to mild drunkenness, and he had emerged into the top of the tower, housing the impressive and ancient mechanism of the church clock, in a disoriented, rather alarmed state. The vicar had been prattling on, trying to inform him of the church's history, but Professor Seabright, in his distressed condition, had not taken in a word of it. He had felt dizzy and sick and panicked, and the stern, iron beat of the clock had seemed to thud through him.

The reverend had made him sit, and after only a moment or two his breathing had steadied and he had felt calm again. In fact, he had soon forgotten about it entirely. But now, in room eleven of the guesthouse, that moment was back with him, and he could hear the ticking of the church clock again, shaking his bones . . .

and the hidden clock,

and the drip of blood,

and the drip of tears.

And his breath, another rhythm adding to the cacophony.

And the beat of his heart, a further pulse, loud and relentless.

"Make it stop!" he pleaded to the still night. "Please make it stop!"

His vision began to blur and darken around the edges. The room receded into blackness, leaving only the notebook in light and focus, a dark bloodstain blooming on the cover, growing from his cut hand. He could hear his heartbeat now above everything else, like a mighty drum, could feel the shudder of it rattling through him, as if his heart was striking hard against the inside of his rib cage with each fierce beat, barging at it as if eager for release.

He shook and he trembled and he rocked.

"Please make it stop!"

As if in answer to this plea, all the noise ceased: the ticking and the dripping and the gasping sobs.

And the heartbeat, too.

The notebook dropped from his hand, but Professor Seabright was not living to hear it hit the floor.

*P*rofessor Cleary smiles broadly, leans back in her chair. It seems to Jack that she looks rather pleased with herself. And, looking at the others, it seems as if she has good reason to be.

The previous stories were greeted with appreciation, certainly, but this one seems to have had a deeper effect on its audience. Some look rather shaken by it—eyes fixed, tight-faced, tense—which, Jack assumes, is the desired response. Only Mr. Osterley seems unmoved, retaining his same detached calm. Amelia, the young girl by Jack's side, is fidgeting more than ever, though. She looks agitated.

"Are you okay?" says Jack.

She glares back at him. "Course. Yes. Fine." But she turns her head quickly away again, as Jack does likewise. He doesn't understand. It didn't seem such a very scary story to him, at least no more so than the others. Has he missed something? Because everyone seems to be dumbstruck.

"Well done, madam," says Mr. Fowler at last. "We seem to be lost for words, so I suppose your words must have struck home."

"Good," says the professor. "I'm so glad you enjoyed it."

"Oh, he didn't say he enjoyed it," says Katy Mulligan, the young woman with the severe-looking haircut. "I'm not sure any of us enjoyed it, Miriam." She fixes a hard look on Professor Cleary. "But I suppose it worked." She gives a small nod.

Professor Cleary grins smugly back at her. "Yes, it served its purpose rather well, I think," she says. "Got to the heart of the matter, as it were."

Katy Mulligan scowls at her, and seems about to say more, but Mr. Osterley quietly cuts in.

"Quite," he says, and though his expression seems unchanged, and his tone of voice is soft and even, there is somehow a firm authority to that one word, and both the professor and Ms. Mulligan fall silent. "Thank you, Professor." A small turn of the wrist and a lazy wave of the hand invite the professor to extinguish her candle.

The professor accepts, blows out the flame with an exaggerated pout, and slides her chair back without a word.

"Very good," says Mr. Osterley. "Perhaps it is time to hear from one of our younger guests now." Jack's chest tightens, but Mr. Osterley, with a typically slight gesture, is indicating the boy to Jack's left: tall, stooping Lee, who nods and mumbles in reply. "Oh, uh . . . yeah. 'Kay." He raises a skinny arm to rest a hand on the back of his neck, as if it is not yet bowed low enough and he might be about to tug it down another few inches. His other hand ruffles through his hair for a moment. "Yeah, well, it's, um . . . odd. It's an odd story but . . . Well, you might not think it's very . . . Anyway . . ."

And then he coughs.

And then he says "Um" again.

And then he begins.

Beneath
the Surface

They all fell into the water when the boat went over, but Jonah was the only one who woke up in the hospital that night. He heard the doctors talking about him when they thought he was asleep.

"He ought to be dead, too. That long under the water . . . It's some kind of miracle."

They didn't show him his parents. And they couldn't show him his brother; they never found him.

Now his aunt and uncle do their best, but they're deadened by grief, and they never wanted children of their own, and it shows. Jonah's room in their house used to be the spare bedroom, and that shows, too. It's as if he's just another guest expected not to outstay his welcome. He tries his best not to get in the way. He helps out with chores. He does his homework quietly in his room. He reads a lot. Sometimes they all watch television together. Comedies, mostly. They like canned laughter on the sound track to remind them when they're meant to laugh. It's too easy to forget otherwise.

They don't talk about Jonah's mum and dad, or his brother. They sleepwalk from day to day. No one seems to notice. Life, or at least something superficially resembling it, goes on.

One day, Jonah is walking home from school along the towpath by the river; he goes this way fairly often, and some of the people who live on the houseboats recognize him and give him a wave and a smile. He comes to a bend in the river where there are no boats, and he's alone on the path when he thinks he sees something move in the water.

He goes over closer to the edge and gazes down. It looks as if the mud at the bottom has been disturbed. It's swirling about in billowing gray clouds that are just beginning to settle, and he sees that fish are swimming away from there, but he can't see what's kicked the mud into motion to begin with. He stares, puzzled for a minute, then turns to go, but slips on the bank, falls onto his front, and his feet slide down the grassy slope into the water.

His legs are submerged as far as his knees before he grabs hold of a mooring post and brings himself to a stop. So then he's lying there feeling foolish and pulling himself back up out of the water, and the wet material of his trousers is clinging to his legs, when something brushes against his foot. A fish or some weed, he supposes, just glancing against him, but enough to make him jump.

He scrambles up the bank a little way and turns to look at the water, his arms clutching his wet knees beneath his chin. The clouds of mud he's stirred up settle, the rippled surface of the water flattens, and everything goes still. And now he's wet, flustered, and embarrassed, as a couple of older girls from his school pass by, giggling. He runs home and races upstairs to change his clothes before his aunt and uncle can see him.

Later they have dinner and make the usual polite chitchat. His uncle's day at work was "fine," his aunt's was "fine," Jonah's day at school was "fine." He doesn't even consider telling them about what happened at the river. He's almost forgotten all about it himself.

Then one day in the following week, it rains during the morning, and when Jonah sets off back home the roads and pavements are still wet. He cuts through the old shopping area where Barker's, the newsstand, used to be. When he was young, he and his brother would buy sweets there when they were visiting Auntie Jane. There are puddles scattered around the parking lot, and in one corner the paving slabs are cracked and tilted, forming a mini lake of rainwater.

Rather than detour around it, Jonah decides to jump it. He takes a running leap, and as he passes over the puddle he catches sight of his reflection in the water. Only it isn't him. It's someone else's face that he sees there, pale and blank, looking up at him with wide eyes. It's his brother—his dead brother—staring up at him out of a gray puddle of water in a rundown shopping mall.

Jonah lands badly, falls painfully to his hands and knees, feels his lungs empty. When he gets up, he

103

doesn't look back at the puddle. He walks away quickly, runs home.

Everyone has had a "fine" day, and his aunt and uncle don't notice his grazed palms. After they've eaten and Jonah has done his homework, they watch a film on television and laugh in all the places where it seems like they ought to.

The next day, Jonah tells his aunt and uncle that he's feeling ill and can't go to school. They don't ask questions, except to check that he'll be all right left alone all day while they're at work. There's a subtle implication that, if needed, one of them will take the day off to be with him. But there's a much less subtle hint that they'd rather not.

Jonah says he'll be fine on his own. Says he'll just read in bed and get some rest, and so they go to work. Then Jonah plays computer games all day, with the sound on headphones, and ignores the noise of the rain against the windows.

A wet weekend passes in a similar fashion. Jonah's aunt and uncle make suggestions for trips out, but he says he's happy to stay in "just to be on the safe side," even though he feels much better, and they're happy to accept this and do their own thing without him.

Monday is sunny and dry and Jonah declares that he has made a full recovery. School is "fine." He gets the bus home for a change, even though walking would probably be quicker. He sits on the top deck near the back, playing games on his phone, and misses his stop.

When he gets off at the next one, it's starting to rain again, even though the forecast on the radio in the morning had said dry all day. It's one of those sudden showers, the kind that goes from nothing to a downpour in a second. The pavement is instantly awash: one vast puddle churned into chaos by the torrent of rain. Jonah runs homeward, eyes ahead, ignoring his fractured reflection beneath him. The street is almost empty of other pedestrians, though it's hard to see for sure through the dense curtain of rain.

He turns a corner and comes to a sudden halt. Directly ahead of him there's a kind of shadow in the falling rain. Only it's not a shadow—it's more of an absence. The hard, straight lines of rain are broken, as if hitting something invisible. It's hard to make out exactly what, but it's a little shorter than Jonah, and roughly the shape of a boy.

"Joe?" he says, and shivers. He hasn't spoken his brother's name since he died, and the taste of it on his lips now is bittersweet. He lifts a hand up slowly. Reaches forward toward the apparition, trembling and expectant.

The kid on the skateboard is a bit younger than Jonah, and going too fast to do anything about it when he rounds the corner and finds himself headed straight toward Jonah's back. Jonah doesn't hear him coming, only feels the impact. He's thrown forward, arms splayed like frantic wings, and lands heavily on the wet paving slabs, adding fresh grazes to his palms. The boy lands on top of him and knocks the wind out of him. He mumbles something that might either be an apology or swearing, and then he's back on his skateboard and speeding away just as recklessly as before.

When Jonah gets up, there's no gap in the rain anymore, just a relentless torrent. *Stair rods*, as his dad used to say. Some of his books have spilled out of his school bag. He should gather them up before they're ruined, but he's too distracted. He's thinking about stair rods and he doesn't know what he's feeling.

At home, everything has been "fine" for everyone, except for the weather. Jonah doesn't feel like trying to laugh at the TV so he goes up early to his room to do homework and read. With headphones on and the music turned up loud, concentrating hard on his book, he barely notices the sound of the rain on the window. He doesn't hear the knock on his door at all. His uncle appears behind it as it swings open.

"We're just nipping out. Jenny called and we're off around to hers for a while. Do you want to come?"

Jenny is a woman a couple of streets away. Jonah is scared of her gigantic dog and her strangely immobile hairstyle. He says he's happy just to stay in and carry on reading. Uncle John seems perfectly happy with this, too.

They've been gone about an hour when the lights go out. Jonah peeps out of the window and sees that the streetlights and the lights in the other houses are still on. He knows there's some kind of fuse box in the basement—the lights had gone out once before a couple of weeks earlier, and Auntie Jane had gone down to reset the switch.

Jonah uses his phone to light his way safely downstairs, gets a proper flashlight from a drawer in the kitchen, and then opens the door to the basement. He's only been down there once before, when he first moved in. He'd brought along more stuff than could fit into his room, so some of it had gone down to the basement temporarily.

The stairs down are narrow and creaky and there's no banister, just a (slightly wobbly) handrail running down the wall, so the other side is open, with the potential for a longish drop if you misstep near the top. It isn't much of a worry when you can see where you're going, but somehow in the darkness it seems much more of a danger. Jonah keeps the flashlight trained studiously on the steps beneath his feet and edges down slowly. When he gets to the bottom step, he notices something strange: the pool of light at the end of the flashlight's beam has ripples in it.

Standing still, he tracks the flashlight over the floor of the basement. It is entirely covered in water. He flicks the flashlight beam up to the back wall. Right near the top there's a small barred window, opening to the outside at ground level. It's been broken for years (the result of a mishap with a cricket ball that Joe and Jonah had each claimed was the other's fault), cracked and holed and letting in torrents of rainwater, directly onto the fuse box.

It takes Jonah a moment to realize what has happened: the river runs through the meadow behind the house; it must have burst its banks, flooding the garden and then leaking into the basement. He points the light around the room, piecing together the full scene from the fragments freed from darkness by its beam. The floor is a shallow sea with islands of all the boxes and junk that are kept down there.

One of those boxes—one of Jonah's boxes—is full of photographs. He decides that before he phones Auntie Jane's cell he'll get the box—full of his past, full of his dead family frozen in life—out of harm's way. A little more scanning around with the flashlight beam finds the particular box in a far corner.

Jonah steps down from the bottom step and moves toward the box. But when he steps out, the floor isn't where it ought to be. Though the water can't be more than a few inches deep, his foot drops ankle-deep beneath the surface, as if going down one more step on the staircase. Thrown off balance, Jonah lurches forward. His other foot goes forward to steady himself—and drops another step down.

But there isn't another step there. Jonah can see boxes across the room that show with certainty the level of the floor. But his feet are beneath it. He is standing shin-deep in less than an inch of water. It makes no sense at all. But he is puzzled rather than alarmed.

Jonah steadies himself as best he can, wobbling and waving his arms. As he does so, the dancing flashlight flits over something else odd happening. In the center of the floor, the water is moving, bulging up in a way that water can't do, forming itself into a tiny hill that continues to rise, grow, and shape itself. He steadies the beam of light to watch it, still strangely calm.

In a few seconds, a bizarre effigy stands before him: water in the shape of a boy. The features are unclear— they ripple and change—but he knows it is his brother.

He knows it is Joe.

The watery figure raises a hand slowly, and Jonah raises his own hand to match it. He looks into his brother's face—his face made of water, which he looks *through* as much as *at*. And he feels something, as he did when he saw the reflection in the puddle, and again when he saw the figure in the rain: it had been fear to begin with, but now it's a sad longing, a slow, long ache of loss.

Then this ghost made of water turns and walks slowly away, and with each step he drops lower in the water, as if the staircase continues on, down below the basement floor.

Jonah follows him, sinking deeper into the water with each pace. As the apparition's head dips beneath the surface Jonah laughs. A real laugh. Then, without really thinking about it, he holds his empty breath, and steps down and down.

Now the water is over his head. And now there is nothing beneath his feet anymore and he drops slowly down, deeper into the impossible water. He lets go of the flashlight and it sinks away from him, still shining, twirling away into distance and darkness. He feels his hands being held: one by soft, slender fingers; one by a larger, rougher hand.

And he laughs again, and water fills his lungs. Somewhere beneath him the flashlight dies, blinking into nothingness, and Jonah sinks happily into the welcoming dark.

*J*ack looks around, and stooping Lee isn't stooping anymore. As he had told his story he had straightened in his chair, his voice had grown stronger, his narration more assured and fluent, as if the story had filled him with new confidence. He even raised his head a little.

If he's not careful he might even reveal his eyes from beneath that ragged fringe. But now, with the story ended, he notices the attention of the others and shrinks back again, folds up, packs himself away from their gaze.

"So, uh, that was . . . Like I said, it's not a very . . . Uh, yeah, um . . ."

"I liked it," says Jack quietly. He doesn't look over at Lee as he says it, and nor does Lee look back when he replies.

"Uh, thanks. Um, yeah . . ." And he seems to shrivel up a little more.

Jack can see from their expressions that the others all seem perfectly satisfied by Lee's story, and his telling of it, but none of them says anything. Perhaps, Jack reasons, that's just the way Lee prefers it, and he curses himself for having said the little that he did.

"Thank you, Lee," says Mr. Osterley, and Lee eagerly blows out his candle and pushes his chair away from the table.

With six of the thirteen candles now extinguished, the light from the remaining flames does not extend as far beyond the confines of the table as it did at the start of the evening. The shadows, previously confined to the edges of the room, are creeping in, like gathering clouds.

Those who have told their stories and withdrawn are just gray shapes now, almost featureless. Jack can barely make out the wall beyond Mr. Osterley. He wonders whether he would still be able to make out the door if he turned around. And he knows it's silly, but he feels the absence of Lee to his left now. With his story told, there are four chairs in a row pushed back around that side now, four candles blown out, four dark figures sitting back in the gloom. It feels like a dark hole has opened up there, and that he'll need to take care not to fall into it. For all her strangeness, he's very glad that Amelia is still there on his right, fidgeting away.

The dark gap reminds Jack, too, that time is running out for him to think of something to say when his own turn comes, but for now his mind feels like just another dark gap.

"Perhaps," says Mr. Osterley, and he pauses for a moment that Jack fills with silent panic, "Ms. Mulligan might tell our next tale this evening?"

Jack hopes that his relief is not too obvious.

Katy Mulligan, with her short, serious haircut and her hard eyes, clasps her hands together in front of her on the tabletop. She's rather small but sits up very straight, looking determined and businesslike.

"Yes," she says.

And that, apparently, is all the introduction she intends to give.

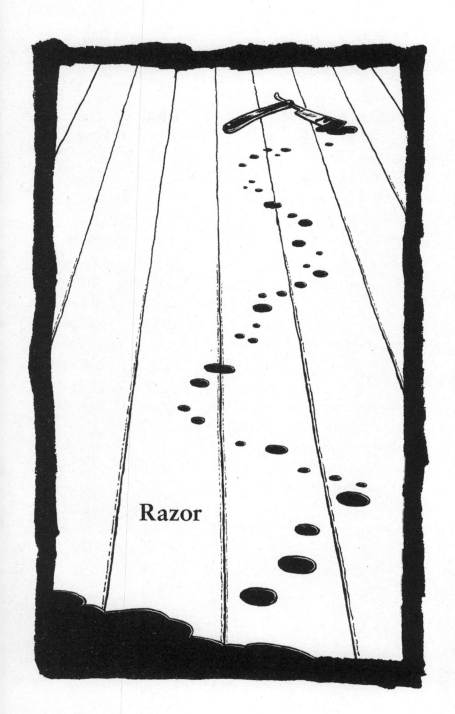

Razor

Never chase a story that starts in a pub. That was pretty much the first bit of advice that Peter's boss had ever given him, back when he started out at the *Dunstable Gazette*. He was very fond of giving advice, that editor, and Peter was fond of ignoring it. But for some reason he'd always taken notice of that one particular warning. At least, he had until now. Because this story, the murder, was the one that had gotten away as far as Peter was concerned.

Peter had joined the *Chronicle* just after the murder story had come to its end. It had been an enormous story for so small a paper: *Local Property Millionaire Murdered in His Own Home*. Peter had picked up the gist of it from conversations with his new colleagues, and read through the back issues to fill in the details: the murder weapon (an old-fashioned cut-throat razor put to fatally literal use); the gory details of the crime scene; some background character stuff on both victim and suspect; the arrest of the wife at Inverness airport; the lengthy trial, conviction, and sentencing. It was a once-in-a-lifetime story for a journalist on a local rag, and Peter had missed it by days.

But then, this lunchtime, there had been the man called Brian in the pub. They had fallen to talking at the bar and it had turned out that Brian ran a specialist cleaning company. He had done some work for a real estate agency in the house where the murder had happened.

And he believed the house to be haunted. Normally Peter would have ignored him and moved quickly away, but he had only just been served his hamburger and fries. He wasn't leaving anytime soon, so he feigned interest and reached for the ketchup.

"Now, don't go thinking I'm some kind of nut," said Brian. "I don't believe in ghosts." He looked down at a beer coaster on the bar, picked it up. "I like science, me. I like things that can be explained, measured, proved. I don't believe in fate, I don't believe in horoscopes, I don't believe in UFOs, I don't believe in alternative medicines, and I certainly don't believe in ghosts." He picked at one corner of the coaster, separating the top layer of paper from those below, keeping his eyes focused on this small task, as if too embarrassed to look at Peter. "The only spirits I believe in are lined up behind the bar." He glanced very briefly at Peter's face, offered up a smile as weak as his joke, then turned his attention back to the coaster, tearing fragments off the corner with nervous, scratching fingers.

"But . . . ?" said Peter, pausing between mouthfuls of burger.

"But there was *something* in that place." Another tiny fragment of torn card dropped to the bar. The coaster looked as if it had been nibbled at by mice now.

116

A moment passed. Peter's smiling expression did not alter. Finally, Brian seemed to make a decision, looked up into Peter's eyes, and held his gaze.

"I was in that place three days. It wasn't just the blood and such that needed cleaning up; the police had been in and out for days and made a right old mess. But I've done these kinds of jobs before, and it doesn't bother me much anymore. But I swear, in that place . . . It sounds corny, I know, but there was this . . . *presence* there. Normally there's two of us does the work, me and a lad. But the lad's off sick so I'm doing this one on my own. The whole time I'm there I'm alone. But it doesn't *feel* like I'm alone."

Peter dipped a thoughtful fry into his ketchup. "Easy to imagine stuff when you know something like that's happened in a place, I would think," he said.

"Maybe," said Brian. "But like I say, I'm used to this kind of thing, more or less. Never bothered me before. Odd thing was, it was all the rooms *except* the one where the murder was."

"Really?" The next fry halted on its way to Peter's mouth as he considered this.

"Yeah. All the time I'm working in the main bedroom, where, y'know . . . all the time I'm in *there*, it's fine. But every other room I feel like there's somebody else there. And it's not as if it feels like anything threatening or bad or anything, but it's still creepy. And I can do without creepy, if I'm honest."

Peter thought Brian probably *was* honest. But it was

all very vague. He'd briefly thought there might be the germ of a story in it, but even with a good dose of his usual enthusiastic embellishment this looked pretty thin.

"And then there was the weird thing with my kit," said Brian.

"Mm-hmm?" said Peter, most of his attention back with his burger now.

"See, the first day I took everything back out at the end of the day and packed it in my van, 'cause I needed it for another little job somewhere else the next morning. Second day I just left everything where it was at the end of the day: vacuum, carpet cleaner, buckets, cloths, sprays, what have you. Needed it there again the next day, so it made sense. When I get in the next morning, though, it's all moved."

"Moved?"

"Yeah. I'd left it all just, y'know, scattered about wherever. Nobody else was gonna be there so I hadn't bothered clearing up. Now it's all tidy. Cloths all folded neatly in piles; bottles and sprays all lined up against one wall, evenly spaced, in order of height; vacuum and carpet cleaner look like new; gleaming, they are. I thought maybe the lad had got better and got in somehow, but no, he's still home in bed. There's only two keys: I've got one, the agency's got the other, and they swear blind nobody's come near the place from there. Well, now I'm proper jumpy about it all, so I finish up the work right quick, and I pack up and get out."

Peter put down his glass with a last mouthful of

beer in it. It still wasn't much of a story. If you looked closely enough there'd probably be a boringly rational explanation. But he'd remembered something that Sally from the news desk had told him about the dead man.

He'd been obsessively tidy.

Properly, clinically obsessive-compulsive. All the tins in the cupboard with the labels facing the same way, all that kind of thing. It'd come out in the trial along with a dozen other odd quirks that had driven his wife nuts. So maybe—if he got an appointment to view the property, and took some sneaky pictures on his camera phone while he was there—he could put together a jolly little two-page spread about it. It was worth a try.

It looked ordinary. That wasn't good.

In fact, it was worse than ordinary. It was nice. And nice was disastrous.

Peter had been hoping that the house might look haunted. He'd imagined something dark, dilapidated, and Gothic; something bleak; something menacing. Window boxes overflowing with perky geraniums really didn't fit the bill. He thought about not bothering at all, but then he saw a ruddy face at the front window, smiling out through the flowers. He figured this must be the posh-sounding bloke from the agency—Justin or Jeremy or Julian, something like that—and decided he might as well take a quick look around now that he was here.

Three stone steps up to the substantial front door and an old-fashioned bell pull. The red-faced man opened the door, smiling widely. He looked even posher than he had sounded on the phone, dressed in a slightly garish tweed three-piece suit (which was surely too heavy for this warm spring day), a striped shirt, and a flowery cravat.

Who wears a cravat these days? I mean, really?

"Ah! Good afternoon! Splendid! Splendid!"

"Hello," said Peter. "I'm a little early . . ."

He offered up his hand, but his host had already turned around and was striding off down the hallway. Peter followed, closing the door behind him. Inside was as disappointing as out: clean, bright walls in good repair, varnished bare wooden floorboards that failed to creak as he walked across them, and no sign of a cobweb anywhere.

"Nice, isn't it?" said the tweedy man as he stopped at a door on his left.

Disastrous, thought Peter.

The man opened the door and Peter followed him into a depressingly cheery, light, spacious, and distinctly unsinister front room.

"Lovely room, this!" said the man, beaming with irritating enthusiasm and gesturing extravagantly with both arms, as if to emphasize the space. "Just beautiful! All the furniture is Edwardian! In terrific condition!"

"Great," said Peter.

He showed polite interest as his tweedy host showed him around the ground floor, but his heart sank further with each moment. Brian seemed to have done an unhelpfully thorough job, leaving each room spotless. And not a hint of anything supernatural, though admittedly, he might have struggled to notice such a thing anyway with Mr. Tweedy accompanying him closely at every step, enthusing about each room with as much pride as if it were his own home.

Peter's last hope was that he could somehow gain some time alone in the bedroom where the murder had taken place, perhaps find some remains of a bloodstain to photograph to add a little spice to his prose. So throughout his tour of the bathroom, study, and guest bedrooms, he tried to think of some excuse to free himself from Mr. Tweedy. But, as it turned out, he needn't have bothered.

"This is the main bedroom." A tweedy sleeve indicated the appropriate door, but the man from the agency made no move to go through it himself.

Tentatively, Peter turned the handle and pushed the door open, expecting his host to follow him in. But he only looked away, somewhat awkwardly, remaining shuffling on the landing as Peter entered. A stroke of luck at last, or so he thought. But here again, Brian had been thoughtlessly diligent. There was not the faintest trace of a bloodstain remaining. And still he felt no mysterious presence.

He looked in vain around the room for something,

anything, that might offer proof of the murder or, even slightly, support the idea of some supernatural presence, but there was nothing. Of course there wasn't. What a waste of time! Peter cursed his own stupidity. He should know better than to chase so flimsy a story.

"Never chase a story that starts in a pub," he muttered. He smiled to himself. What had he expected anyway? To meet the ghost in person and sign him up for an exclusive interview?

"Ha!" Peter laughed at his own ridiculousness.

"Is everything all right?"

Peter turned to face the doorway. Tweedy was still out on the landing.

"Yes, everything is fine. Thank you."

He had a thought: Tweedy was obviously not coming into the bedroom because he was spooked by what had happened there. But he hadn't mentioned anything about the murder, naturally. Plenty of detail about the lovely Edwardian furniture and the original architectural features but, oddly, no information about the recent—and very bloody—murder. Typical real estate agent! But if he was spooked about the room then maybe there was a particular reason. Maybe *he* had seen or felt something in there. Worth asking him a question or two, at least. Give him a bit of a push.

"It's a lovely house," said Peter.

"Thank you," came the reply from the landing.

"But, well"—Peter moved toward the doorway so that he could see out to Tweedy, shuffling awkwardly, his eyes studiously averted—"to be blunt, I'm surprised you haven't lowered the rent, under the circumstances."

"The rent? I don't . . ." Tweedy looked uneasy, almost confused. Still he faced away from the bedroom.

"It's just that, well, I would have thought that what happened here might put a lot of people off."

" 'What happened'? I'm sorry, but what do you mean, 'what happened'?"

Oh, don't try to play the innocent.

"I mean the murder, obviously. The murder that happened here."

Not subtle, but perhaps he could shock something out of this odd little man.

"Murder?" Mr. Tweedy half turned his head in Peter's direction now, and managed a fair impression of dumb surprise.

"Yes, murder. I would have thought something like that might make you put the rent down a bit."

"Murder?" He was really nervous now, staring down at the floor.

Caught out, thought Peter. *You're not so chatty now, are you?* Encouraged, he pressed harder. "Blood everywhere. Throat slit with a cut-throat razor. Don't tell me you didn't know."

But looking at him closely now, the tweedy man really did seem genuinely shocked, and Peter realized he had pushed too hard. The poor man was shaking now, his eyes wide, his mouth half open, trembling. His fingers nervously fidgeting at his ridiculous cravat.

"Did you say a *cut-throat razor?*"

An old-fashioned cut-throat razor.

Who uses a cut-throat razor these days?

I mean, really?

The man in the tweed suit—who, now that he thought about it, did not sound very much at all like the agent Peter had spoken to on the phone earlier—was very pale now. He had finally turned his head, with great effort, forcing himself to look into the bedroom.

"I forgot," he said.

His face quite blank, he shuffled past Peter into the room. There was a dressing table in the far corner and he slumped into the chair before it and stared, horrified, at his reflection in the mirror. Peter watched him, dumbstruck by realization.

His phone rang. Keeping his eyes fixed unwaveringly on the seated figure at the dressing table, he answered it.

"Hello?"

"Hello. Mr. Watson?"

Peter recognized the voice at once. "Yes," he whispered, transfixed, as the man in the tweed suit, still staring into the mirror, raised trembling hands to his face and gently traced inquisitive fingers across his features.

"This is Jolyon, from Burlingham Real Estate? I was just phoning to say I'm so sorry that I'm not there yet to let you in. I'm afraid I'm stuck in traffic. I do hope you've not been—"

Peter ended the call. His hand dropped to his side and the phone fell to the bare wooden floorboards with a thump.

"How could I forget?" said the man at the dressing table. He dropped his shaking hands to his neck and Peter watched his reflected face, his pale fingers fluttering at the cravat, fumblingly loosening it. "How could I forget such a thing?"

There was something dark and wet on his fingertips. His face was a terrible picture of horrified remembrance. The cravat was nearly loose now. He hooked two dripping fingers behind it and began to pull.

Peter wanted to beg him to stop, but he could not speak. Nor move. He could only watch. He knew beyond all doubt exactly what the next moment held.

And he wished that he could look away.

*I*t's colder now. It's later in the evening, so of course it's colder, but that's not why Jack shivers. His imagination is telling him the story beyond the ending, and he doesn't like what his mind's eye sees. His eyes have lost all focus for a moment but then he's jolted out of his daze by a small, sharp cry.

His eyes focus on the source of the shriek. Something is wrong with kindly, welcoming Frances Crane. Her arms are crossed tightly over her chest, her head has dropped forward, and she is rocking as she takes in short jabs of breath, each one accompanied by a high whistling sound. When she lifts her head, her handsome face is distorted by distress, her laugh lines full of tears. And then all of those tiny gasped-in breaths are released in one mighty, wailing sob. Her arms unfold and she drops her palms flat on the table, as if she's bracing herself, and gentle Frances Crane cries out a raw animal sound that rings around the room.

Jack stares wide-eyed at her, scared and upset and confused. Katy Mulligan is staring at her, too, her neatly painted lips parted in alarm.

"Frances," she says. "Oh my God, what is it? What—"

Then Frances Crane lifts a hand to her head, clamping the palm to her temple, and as she does so her bangles and the wide sleeve of her blouse drop down away from her wrist to reveal an ugly scrawl of heavy, dark scars crisscrossing the skin. Jack gasps at the sight of it—he can't help himself—and Frances's reaction is

immediate. She drops her hand quickly out of sight,
pulling her sleeve back into place, and tries to regain
control of her breathing. But Katy Mulligan, at least,
has seen the scars, too. She looks horrified.

"Oh God, Frances, I'm so sorry. I had no idea. If I'd
known I would never—"

Frances pulls a fragile smile into place and, with great
care, wipes tears away. "No, of course not, Katy. There's
no reason you should have known. Don't mind me."
She sniffs. "Don't mind me, everybody." She beams
around at those still seated in the light, and those back
in the shadows, too. "That just . . . got the better of me
for a moment. So sorry. But it only goes to show what a
fine story it was, Katy. You should be proud. Really
you should." She aims her best and bravest reassuring
smile over at Katy, whose mouth has clamped shut tight
now, her face a picture of tense sympathy. She seems
about to say something more, but the pale man cuts in.

"Thank you, Ms. Mulligan," he says, and there is no
drama in his voice, no emotion, no sympathy really, but
somehow his blank tone is calming anyway. Katy, after
one last glance at Frances, blows out her candle and
lifts her chair back into the darkness without another
word. Jack is still in shock. He knows what those marks
must mean, but he can't quite believe it. Frances seems
so happy, jolly, positive; surely she would never . . .

And they were livid scars, too, from deep cuts made
with force and effort and intent. It's a wonder that she

survived. And now Jack is thinking things he doesn't
want to think again, and as he does so he is staring into
space. Only he realizes he is staring into space in the
direction of Frances Crane, which must look like he's
simply gawping at her. He turns his head away and
finds himself now looking at Amelia, by his side, who is
apparently entirely unworried by the sight of Frances's
savaged wrist. She is singing happily to herself under
her breath and swaying in time with her own music.

"Amelia," says Mr. Osterley. She looks up.

"Is it my turn now?"

"Yes, Amelia."

"Good. Because I have a story to tell that is a true
story about me. It is from when I was at school. Before.
And it is a good story and I think you will like it and I
will tell it to you now."

And she does.

The Girl in the Red Coat

D id you see that?"
Charley is talking to me and pointing over to the green wire fence at the far end of the playground. This is strange. Charley doesn't normally talk to me. Charley is loud and cheeky and funny and popular, and he normally mainly talks to Zack and Kazim, who are also loud and funny and popular, and to Callum, who is loud.

I am not loud or funny or cheeky or popular. I am quite clever and quiet and not cool, and the other children make fun of my glasses, which are held together by Scotch tape at the moment because Dad fixed them with not very good glue in a hurry after Ellie sat on them, and so they broke again really easily when Sam kicked a football in my face, which was an accident again. And Dad is going to get some better glue and fix them better and then maybe, maybe, we'll see, get me some new glasses soon.

And because I am not popular or cool, Charley does not talk to me. Ever. But Charley is talking to me now and pointing over to the green wire fence at the far end of the playground, but all I can see over there is the fence and some fallen leaves and some rubbish. There aren't many other children here yet, just me and Charley and Callum and a girl in a red duffle coat. Dad drops me off early on the way to his work so I'm normally one of the first three earliest to arrive out of the whole school.

"Do you mean the potato chip bag?" I say.

But when I look back, Charley isn't there anymore. He is running off the other way behind Callum, and they are both laughing, and Callum is carrying something. And I look at the ground down to my left and my bag isn't there, even though that is where I put it down, and I realize that the thing that Callum is carrying is my bag, and they're running away with my bag with my lunch and my PE clothes and my water bottle and my homework in it.

"Hey!"

I run after them. I am quite good at running and I am not carrying any bags, and Charley is carrying a bag and Callum is carrying two bags (including mine), so I catch up with them.

"Hey! Give it back!"

I am in front of Charley and behind Callum, and before I catch up to Callum, he turns around and throws my bag over my head. Then Charley catches it and stops running and sort of shakes it about in front of him a bit as if he's dancing with it. I have stopped running, too, and I turn to face Charley, so now Callum is behind me.

"Ha-ha!" says Callum. "Piggy in the middle!"

"Give me back my bag, please, Charley," I say to Charley—which is polite, even though Charley has not been polite to me, but I am setting him a Good Example—and I walk toward him with my arms out. And Charley holds the bag out straight toward my hands, but when I try to take it, he pulls it back again and then throws it over my head to Callum again. And now I am really annoyed.

"Piggy in the middle," says Callum. "Oink, oink!"

And I think this is a very silly thing to say. It is a horrible thing when Callum calls Neelam a pig, because Neelam is a bit fat and it makes her cry sometimes when Callum calls her a pig. But it is not a horrible thing to say to me because I am not fat at all. I am nine years old, but I am small and thin and wear clothes that I get Dad to cut the labels out of so that no one sees that they are meant to be for seven-year-olds.

If Callum wants to try to make me cry he should call me something to do with being little, like "titch" or "stick insect" or something, because that would make more sense (even though it still wouldn't make me cry because I don't care about that sort of thing because I have a Positive Self-Image because Dad told me I should). So when I punch Callum hard in the tummy and he throws up onto his shoes (which are those silly sneakers with the flashing lights, which you aren't even meant to wear at school anyway), it's not because he has called me a piggy in the middle; it's just that Callum and Charley are taller than me

133

and could carry on throwing my bag over me for ages and I want it back before my sandwiches get all messed up because Dad made me ham and cheese and tomato ones this morning and the tomatoes get messy really easily if you're not careful (and Callum and Charley were definitely NOT being careful) so I made them stop.

I walk over to Charley. His eyes are very wide and his mouth is open and he looks funny. I take my bag off him and he doesn't say anything because I am quiet and clever and he didn't expect that I might hit anybody in the tummy and make them cry and throw up over their shoes so he is surprised.

I am a bit surprised, too, actually. And when I get called into Mrs. Brock's office (Mrs. Brock is our head-mistress), she tells me that she is surprised, too. She says she is "surprised and disappointed." She tells me that it is not allowed to punch children in the tummy, even if they are Callum Yates, and even if it is to protect your sandwiches, which have tomatoes in them. She says it in her stern voice that she uses in assembly for Serious Announcements, but she is smiling quite a lot, too, so I think I am not in too much trouble.

I think it helps that none of the teachers like Callum, because he is probably the naughtiest child in our year and probably number three in the whole school, after Jenny Blake who was caught smoking and Luke Kelly who set off a firework in the boys' bathroom and everybody is scared of. I look at the floor and say,

"Sorry, Mrs. Brock," and she says, "Well, okay, then," and sends me back to my classroom.

It is interesting walking along the corridors when lessons have already started and the corridors are all empty. Normally there is everybody else laughing and chatting and shouting, but now there is only the sound of my shoes going *click-clack click-clack* as I walk quickly because it is math now and I am missing it, and I like math because it is interesting and I am good at it.

My school shoes are probably my noisiest shoes, and because there is only me in the corridor they sound extra noisy and they echo a bit and it sounds good. And because it is good I lift my knees up high as I walk and stomp along extra loudly in the bits of corridor that aren't too close to classrooms that have strict teachers in them. My teacher is Miss Khosla, and she is nice because she is only three-and-a-half-out-of-ten strict, so I am quite loud in the last bit of corridor up to quite close to her door, then I walk along the last bit normally.

Now that I am outside the door, I think that it is not a clever thing to punch the naughtiest boy of the year in the tummy because he will probably want to do revenge on me. Abby told me that Callum made her eat a spider once. And that was for *no reason*; not because he was doing revenge on her. So I am a bit worried now and I just stand still outside the door for a little bit.

And then I hear somebody else's noisy shoes somewhere, and so I know that somebody else must be out of class, too, and I wonder if they have been sent to be told off, too. I look back along the corridor to where I think I can hear it coming from and I think I see the girl in the red duffle coat disappearing past the corner. I wonder if she is new at school because I don't think I have seen her before today. And now I can't hear her noisy shoes anymore, but I've forgotten about thinking about Callum and revenge so I turn the door handle and go into the classroom.

When I go in all the other children go "Wooooo!" like they always do when somebody has been to see Mrs. Brock, only Callum doesn't join in, and Miss Khosla says, "Settle down, class," and tells me to sit down and I sit down in my usual place between Nadia and Imran, and Nadia is trying really hard not to giggle and Imran puts his hands in front of his face like he's going "Don't hit me!" and pretending to be really scared of me and I think about kicking him under the table, just a little bit, but I decide not to.

And then we're doing math, which I like because I'm good at it, but today I pretend not to be quite so good at it because everybody thinks I'm strange and too clever. I help Nadia when she gets stuck, but I don't put my hand up too much when Miss Khosla asks the class questions, and I don't look over at Callum's table hardly at all, so if he is looking at me all scary I don't see it, and so it's okay.

At morning break it is raining, which means we stay inside. Nadia and Kirsten play Single Moms and they ask if I would like to play and I can be Kirsten's baby, Tyrone, if I want, but I say no thank you because I want to read the rainy-day comics. I get one from the box and I go and sit with my back to the window quite near to Miss Khosla's desk where she is doing some marking and drinking tea from a thermos flask, because then if Callum tries to do revenge he can't sneak up behind me and Miss Khosla will see.

I like to play hopscotch or skipping in normal breaks because of the counting and songs, or I like to be alone and pretend things, but on rainy-day breaks I like to read comics.

There is a big box of them and they are very old, which means they have more words and pictures on the pages and hardly any colors. But the one I'm reading is a little bit annoying. I think the comics must have been given to the summer festival by somebody's grandma or something and then the ones that didn't get sold ended up here. And all the stories are in lots of episodes but most times the comic with the next episode in it isn't there, so I just have to read the next one I can find and try to guess what happened in between.

I don't mind too much normally, but this time I realize this comic comes between two that I've read before and now all the things that are happening in the story about the girls in the spooky school are different to everything I made up and it's making me a bit annoyed, partly because some of it isn't as good as what I made up and partly because I'm angry that the comics were in the box in the wrong order even though I spent ages last week sorting them out.

I put down the comic and scowl at Charley, because I decide it might be his fault, and he looks at me a bit funny, only he's not quite looking at me, he's sort of looking over my shoulder, so I look around and there's someone outside the window.

It's a girl, but she's facing away from me, and the window is quite high, so I can only see the back of her head. Her hair is straight and shiny and ginger. I wonder why she's outside in the rain, but then a ball of wadded-up paper bounces off my head (and Miss Khosla doesn't even notice because she's looking at her cell phone) and I turn to make a face at Charley for throwing it, and then when I turn back around the girl is gone.

Then Miss Khosla puts her phone away and blows her nose and says break is over and it's time for the spelling test and I get nine out of ten (because I deliberately get *population* wrong).

Normally I look forward to lunchtime, but today I don't look forward to lunchtime. I don't look forward to it because the rain has stopped now and so we have to go outside and I think that Callum will try to do revenge on me. It's only Mrs. Fleet on duty on the playground today and it's easy to get away with things when it's Mrs. Fleet because she is only one-out-of-ten strict, and I think my sandwiches might be soggy.

When the bell goes, I go and get my lunch box and

138

open it and look inside and I can see that my sandwiches *are* soggy. And because I was right about that I
think I am probably right about Callum, too, so I go
and stand near to Mrs. Fleet to eat my lunch, but she
keeps moving about and it's hard to eat my lunch with
only one hand (because I'm holding my lunch box
with the other), and all the sandwiches are wrapped in
plastic wrap because that's the way I like them so that
even when they get squished I don't get squishy toma-
toness on everything else.

I really need both hands to unwrap the plastic
wrap, so I stop trying to follow Mrs. Fleet around and
sit on the bench by the office and just try to eat my
lunch as fast as I can while Callum and Charley are
busy telling jokes from TV to Fahreed from the next
year up.

I try to keep an eye on them, but I drop some tomato
on my cookies (Dad gave me cookies today because
it is a Wednesday and Wednesdays are cookie days,
and Mondays and Fridays are, too, and Tuesdays and
Thursdays are Healthy Choice days), and so I have to
pay attention to that and get the seeds and juice off the
top cookie as fast as possible to stop it from being too
tomatoey to eat (the bottom one is absolutely fine). I'm
just deciding that the top cookie is not okay to eat
because it will be too tomatoey, but that from now on
I'll ask Dad to wrap the cookies in plastic wrap as well
for extra safety, when I realize that I can't see Mrs.
Fleet at all anymore. But I can see Fahreed from the

next year up and he is not talking to Callum and Charley anymore. Where have they gone?

And what's that smell?

I look down at the ground to my right and see Callum's sneakers with the stupid twinkly lights.

"Your shoes smell like vomit," I say.

"Shut up!" says Callum, and because his mouth is all twisted up, a little bit of spit comes out when he says it and lands on the stain on his shoe. Maybe it will wash it off a bit. He gives me a shove on the shoulder that makes me drop the cookie, the non-tomatoey one, onto the ground, and now it is broken and dirty and I don't have a good cookie left.

"Hey!" I say, but it doesn't sound as brave as I want it to.

Callum hunches up his shoulders and screws up his fists and his face. "I'm going to get you!" he says.

"No, you're not," says somebody else.

I look up and it's a girl I don't recognize. At least, I think I haven't seen her at school before, but she does look a bit familiar. She's wearing the old school uniform that they used to have here ages ago but that they made "optional." ("Optional" means you only wear it if you have crazy parents who want you to be bullied. At least, this is what Dad told me when I asked if I could have one.) She is also wearing a red duffle coat, so I realize that this is the girl who was here earlier.

Her haircut is funny. She has quite long, straight, shiny red hair and it flops down over one side of her face, covering it up completely so you can only see one of her eyes. She is not as tall as Callum and she is quite skinny-looking, but there is something odd about her and her head is tilted down so that the one eye that you can see is looking up through her eyebrow and her body is all sort of stiff and tense and that makes her look a bit scary even though she is only little.

You can tell Callum thinks she looks scary, but he is trying not to let it show, but he does look scared of her and he can't even think up anything to say.

"Yeah, well, just . . ." he says, and points at me. Only he doesn't even properly point at me. He sticks out a finger but he just sort of waves it roughly in my direction, like he's scared that if he actually, properly aims it at me he'll get in trouble with Red Duffle Coat Girl.

I think he's probably right.

He mumbles something and flicks his eyes my way really really quickly one last time, but he's already shuffling away. Then he runs off to tackle a football from Nadia's little brother from kindergarten and nearly trips himself over, which makes me laugh even though he doesn't actually fall over (which would be really funny), but I suppose I laugh a bit extra because I am relieved.

I turn around to thank the girl, but she is walking away, and seeing her head from behind I realize that as well as being the girl who was here earlier, she is also the girl who was outside the window at break time.

I shout after her but she doesn't look back. Then she turns a corner and I think about running after her but I don't run after her because I'm still picking up my lunch.

I eat the tomatoey cookie after all. It is a bit peculiar, but it is okay.

In the afternoon we have science (which I like) and PE (which I don't like unless it is running, and today it is not running, it is indoor exercise, and that is quite bad).

At home time Auntie Anna meets me at school and we walk home and it is not raining. Auntie Anna asks me how was school and I say it was good because of science and I don't mention the strange girl or punching Callum and we stop at the supermarket for Auntie Anna to do a bit of shopping and she buys me a chocolate bar, which I eat and it is nice.

At home, I do my homework and I play a game on Dad's computer. I play Boxworld, which is a puzzle game and doesn't have shooting or zombies in it and I am good at it. I score 13,024 points, which is my second-best score ever (my best score was 16,712 points, but that was when I played for a whole Saturday when the babysitter who we don't have anymore looked after me and didn't stop me and my eyes and my head went a bit funny). Then Dad gets home from work and we have dinner, which is sausages with onion gravy and mashed potato and peas, which is my third favorite dinner, and Auntie Anna stays and eats with us, then goes home.

While we are watching TV, I draw in my special notebook with my good felt-tip pens that I got for my birthday. I draw a police lady (because there is a police lady in the program), and I draw Dad and I draw a cat eating a fish (but I get the mouth a bit wrong). Then I turn the page and I draw the girl in the red duffle coat. I concentrate really hard. I remember the way her hair was and I try to get that right, and I do her uniform and her coat and it all comes out looking quite good. In fact, it's probably one of my top ten best drawings that I've ever done and I am really pleased. I am just finishing coloring in her coat when the man who had done the bad thing at the start of the program is caught by the police lady and the story finishes.

Dad says, "Right then, monster, you should really be in bed by now, you know."

I say, "Can I just finish—"

And then I make a funny squeaky yelping noise because Dad has dropped his not-quite-finished mug of tea and it has spilled on the carpet, and even though the mug has not smashed into smithereens, it is still a big surprise. And when I look up at Dad's face, his eyes are all wide, which I think is being frightened and that makes me a bit frightened. Then, when he sees me being frightened, Dad makes his face into a different shape, I think because he doesn't want to worry me. He worries a lot about not wanting me to worry but really I don't worry much anyway.

"Oops-a-daisy!" says Dad in his not-quite-right

jolly voice, and he smiles at me with his not-quite-right smile. "I'd better get a cloth." And he goes to the kitchen and gets a damp cloth and kneels on the floor mopping up the little bit of tea he spilled. I don't say anything and I stay on the sofa, pretending to watch the ads on the TV but glancing at Dad sometimes and at my drawing sometimes and thinking about what just happened. It is like a puzzle and I like puzzles mostly, except when I can't work them out and they make my head feel funny, and I think this might be one of those ones.

"There we go," says Dad, looking up from the wet patch on the carpet. "I think that'll be okay once it dries." Then he looks at me, and I realize I'm looking at him with a very frowny face from thinking about the puzzle and it puts him off from acting like nothing has happened.

"Sorry, darling," he says. "Your drawing reminded me of something. Something . . . not very nice. It just gave me a bit of a shock, that's all. It's a very good drawing, though. I like . . . I like her red coat." And he smiles at me again, but it's still not a very good one.

"Who does she remind you of, Daddy?" I say. Normally I call Dad "Dad," but when I want something I call him "Daddy" because that works better. I look straight into his eyes with my eyes opened really wide and I keep my mouth tightly closed. Dad's eyes are blinking and he looks in lots of different directions but not really at me.

"A girl named Karen, darling. Karen Hockney. You remember I told you about Susan Hockney, Mummy's friend? Well, Karen was her daughter."

"Oh. The lady and the girl who were in the car with Mummy?"

Daddy is still kneeling on the floor, but he's shuffled over to me now and he's put his arm around me. He thinks I might get upset talking about Mummy and the crash.

"Yes, darling. Mummy was giving them a lift into town." His voice has gone all quiet and full of breath and his eyes aren't blinking anymore. He's looking at me sort of sideways and his eyebrows have gone high up.

"Oh . . ." I say, and look down at the floor and I stay very still and quiet. Sometimes before when I've done this, he's made me hot chocolate and given me cookies. It works this time, too. I even get marshmallow bits in the hot chocolate.

Mostly I don't get upset about Mummy or the crash anymore, not really. Sometimes one of the children at school will say something horrible that makes me feel a bit sad for a little while, but really I don't remember Mummy properly (I was three and a half when the accident happened to her). There are photos of her in the house, though, so I remember what she looked like from them (even though some of them are from before I was born). But mostly the crash is A Thing That Happened and I don't mind it. But I don't talk about it because it makes Dad's eyes go wet.

I ask Daddy if I can play on the computer for ten more minutes before bed and he looks at me carefully and then says, "Well, oooookay then," (which I knew he would) and goes into the kitchen to do the washing up.

I go to the computer but I do not play Boxworld this time because I told Dad a fib and what I really do is go on the Internet and try to find out about Karen Hockney. It is easy. I go on Google and do a search on "susan karen hockney crash" and I find the story from the local newspaper from the day after the crash.

Mostly it tells me things Dad has already told me (only he had never told me that the accident was a *tragic* accident—I thought it was a *traffic* accident). Mummy and the man in the other car died instantly and they get her name wrong, and Susan and Karen Hockney went to the hospital. Then next I find a story from the paper from a day later and Mummy is still dead but they get her name right this time, and now Susan Hockney has died in the hospital, too, and Karen has "serious injuries" but is "stable." And there are photographs of Mummy and the man from the other car and Susan Hockney and Karen Hockney, and the one of Karen Hockney does look a lot like the girl in the red duffle coat, only younger and with her hair different so you can see all of her face. I can see why my drawing would make Dad jump. He gets more upset about Mummy than I do. I suppose that is because he knew her for longer.

In the morning, Dad has toast and horrible coffee for breakfast and I have orange juice and Rice Krispies (because it is Thursday).

"Do you know where she is now?" I say.

Dad lowers his newspaper, which he is reading the back page of with a screwed-up face. "Where who is?" he says.

"Karen Hockney," I say. I have been thinking about Karen Hockney from the moment I woke up.

Dad puts his newspaper down and stares at me for two seconds. Then he puts down his coffee mug (the "World's Fourth Best Dad" one that I got him for his birthday) and stares at me for three more seconds.

"She died, love," he says in his slow, quiet voice that he uses when he thinks he needs to be careful.

"Oh," I say. "I thought she was only seriously injured."

Dad looks at me a bit funny, but doesn't ask any awkward questions. "Yes, she survived the crash," he says. "But she died a few months later. She, um . . ." I think he doesn't know how much he should tell me because he is still wanting to be careful. I look at him with no blinks and guess at how much of a smile is the right amount to make him carry on. I must get it right.

"Karen lost an eye, darling. She had broken bones and her face was very badly cut and one of her eyes . . . got very badly damaged. But she survived and the doctors did some operations on her and she was getting better.

"But then, after another operation . . ." Dad is wriggling about in his chair now, like he needs to go pee or something, but I know he can't need to go pee because he's only just gone (I heard the toilet flush while I was getting the milk out of the fridge). "There were complications. Infection. And Karen got very sick . . . and she died." He stares at me very hard. His mouth has gone all small, and his forehead is wrinkly, but at least he's not wriggling about anymore. I give a little smile to make him see I'm all right.

"How old was she when she died?" I say.

"Oh, um, let's see . . . she was about a year older than you are now when . . . when the crash happened." Dad swallows really loudly, even though he hasn't touched his toast or coffee in ages. "And . . . and she died about a year after that. Yes. So she would have been eleven, I think."

"What was she like?" I say.

"Oh," says Dad. "I don't really know. I think maybe she was quite like her mummy. You remember I told you before how Mummy and Susan were best friends and always looked after each other? Well, I think probably Karen was like that: kind and generous and brave. Darling, why are—"

"What's in my sandwiches today?" I say.

Dad's mouth stops being tight and he smiles a bit, and his forehead goes flat, nearly.

"Tuna and mayonnaise today, love. And an apple and a banana."

I knew that already really (because it is Thursday). "Come on. It's time we were off."

When I get to school, there's Charley and Callum and Harry, from first grade, in the playground. Charley is kicking a tennis ball against the wall and Callum is prodding Harry, but he stops prodding Harry when he sees me. He comes over to me, trying to stomp scarily, which he's not very good at. But he does look very angry with me and that is a bit scary.

I want to say something to try to calm him down a bit but he puts his hand over my mouth. I don't like that at all—I would bite his hand, but I don't want to get ill. Callum is pushing me backward with his hand on my mouth and with his other hand on my shoulder. I stumble backward and fall over and I think I tear my skirt and I hurt my bottom. And now Callum is looming over me and he isn't saying anything, which just makes it scarier. He has clenched his fists up really tightly and he's breathing really noisily and there's a little bit of spit at the corner of his mouth. And I kind of know that he's not really going to kill me, but I still kind of think that he might.

I scuttle along the ground like a crab or something (only a crab that goes backward and not sideways), and Callum follows me but quite slowly. His eyes look really mad. But I'm going faster than him so at least I'm getting a little bit farther away from him. And I think I should get up and run away from him and find a teacher but now I've scuttled backward into somebody's legs so I've stopped and fallen down onto my bottom again. I think at first that they must be Charley's legs, but then I see that Charley is still over by the wall, trying to get his tennis ball out of a drain.

Then the girl from yesterday steps past me to stand between me and Callum.

"Get out of my way!" says Callum. He sounds a bit mad.

The girl just stands there, looking at him.

My bottom really hurts. Maybe I've broken my bottom bone. I try to look at my bottom to check but it's too tricky. When I look up again I can see that the girl has stepped toward Callum and pulled back her hair from her face and Callum has gone white and his eyes are very wide-open. I think probably this is because of how the girl's face looks, because of what the complications and infection must have done to it, but I can only see the back of her head so I can't be sure.

Callum is crying now and his breathing has gone funny like he's forgotten how it works. It's like each breath in is much bigger than the next breath out and so he is inflating. And his face has gone very white and he is shaking. Charley is still over by the wall, but he is looking over at Callum now and he keeps taking one step toward him and then one step back again, over and over, and it looks like a funny little dance.

And he has the dirty yellow tennis ball in his hand and it looks like he's squeezing it very tight.

And now I think Callum has wet himself and I wonder if the puddle of wee he's standing in will make the lights in his sneakers stop working, but I don't think it will. And then he falls down onto his bottom into the puddle of wee and he's making funny wheezing noises and his face is all screwed up.

And I don't think he'll try to do revenge on me now.

The girl turns around and smiles at me and holds out her hand to help me up. She had already let go of her hair so her face is half covered up again now and I can't see what Callum saw, and I think that is a shame because I think it would be interesting to see.

Maybe I will ask her to show me later. I think we might be friends.

*A*melia rocks gently from side to side, humming to herself. She pays no attention to the reaction of the others to her story; instead, she focuses on her candle flame, staring at it with her head cocked to one side.

Jack looks at her, this odd little girl, and thinks about her story. He thinks it was silly of her to say it was a true story, something that had actually happened to her, but then she is young. It's the sort of thing a kid would say, to try to make a ghost story scarier, but Jack's too old for that kind of nonsense. He's seen right through it. What is scaring him, though, is how few people there are left to tell a story, and how he still hasn't thought of anything for his turn. Maybe it'll be all right, he tells himself. He'll think of something when the time comes. He's like this with his English homework sometimes, too. He always leaves it to the last minute, but he comes up with something in the end. And it usually works out okay. Usually.

"That was wonderful," says Frances Crane, just a little too enthusiastically, her eyes shining in the candlelight.

"Really wonderful."

"Thankyouverymuch," says Amelia in a dead tone, without looking up from the flame.

"Amelia?" says Mr. Osterley.

"Uh?"

Mr. Osterley indicates Amelia's candle with first a small hand gesture and then a more expansive one.

Amelia fails to respond to either of them. Then Mr.
Osterley coughs a small, controlled, but perfectly clear
cough that likewise has no effect.

"Amelia, dear," says Frances, and Amelia's attention
flickers briefly in her direction. "Blow out the candle,
will you, please, my love?"

"Oh. Yes. 'Kay. Sorry." After one last lingering
look into the dancing flame, Amelia blows it out
with a short, sharp breath, and then scrapes her chair
awkwardly away from the table.

"Thank you, Miss Crane," says the pale man.
"Thank you, Amelia."

Five candles left. Jack looks over at those others
remaining seated at the table. Four of them all in a line,
more or less opposite Jack: ragged-faced Mr. Fowler,
pale Mr. Osterley, cold and silent Mr. Randolph, and
Frances Crane with laugh lines on her face and scars
on her wrists. And Jack by himself behind his own
lonely candle. It's hard not to imagine that they're all
watching him now, their faces eerie in the candlelight,
staring at him.

Mr. Osterley raises a hand from its place on the table
and turns it slowly at the wrist, his fingers splaying, the
index finger stretching and pointing, pointing, pointing
straight at Jack. His heart lurches, but Mr. Osterley's
hand continues to turn, and his finger moves on, now
vaguely indicating the figure on his right-hand side.

"Mr. Fowler," says the pale man without turning his

153

head. "*Perhaps it is time for you to share another of your tales with us.*"

Mr. Fowler smiles. "*Why, of course, sir, I'll be glad to. And it's a special tale I have for you tonight, for it is not just one of the many that I picked up on my travels, but instead a more . . . personal story, that I seldom share. A tale from my own boyhood. Why indeed, from when I was about the age of this young fellow, I should think.*" He raises an arm in Jack's direction and fashions a wide smile on that craggy face of his. "*It is a dark tale.*" He narrows his eyes. "*A dark tale as perhaps only belongs in childhood.*" He seems now to be speaking only to Jack, his rich, cracked voice mesmerizing. "*And it is a tale within a tale.*"

Mr. Fowler's candlelit face seems to Jack to be floating in the darkness. It is all that he can see.

"*Darkness inside darkness,*" says Mr. Fowler.

Then he begins.

The Patchwork Sailor

D arkness," my uncle liked to tell me, "is good for business."

I thought at first that this was just an excuse for his miserliness. I thought that he was simply unwilling to burn sufficient candles and lamp oil to keep his tavern well lit. But I soon saw for myself that it was true.

"See, this is a sailors' inn," he told me, "and a man who has been to sea has likely as not gathered some secrets to him on his voyages. And he may want those secrets to remain in darkness. So let them as wants to be seen go sit by the fire. Everywhere else . . . well, there should be light enough that if any man should kill another then he can be sure of his identity, but no more than that."

My uncle, like my late father, had been a seafaring man himself in his day, and so had a good knowledge of the ways of sailors. And, indeed, his judgment proved sound. In the port town we had made our home, The Seven Stars was by far the most popular hostelry with seafaring folk, and the simple bill of fare of rum, ale, stew, and darkness (and a strong possibility of a decent brawl) proved both popular and profitable. My uncle, having married my mother shortly after my father's death, regarded me as his rightful property, and so he set me to work in the inn. I worked a little in the kitchen, though this was principally my uncle's domain, having himself been a ship's cook in his sailing days, but mostly I served at tables, and seldom was trade so quiet that I was not worn ragged by the end of the night.

Occasionally, though, a brief respite from my labors might be gained when a lone sailor, in want of an audience for some unlikely tale, bade me join him at his table. I suppose, as I was young, that such men thought me more likely to be gullible and so to believe even their most incredible yarns, and my situation as an employee of the house forced me to maintain a polite silence even when I did not. But from time to time there would be a worthwhile story, well told, that rewarded my attention. Occasionally there may even have been a grain of truth in some of them.

One November evening, in my thirteenth year, it seemed as if just such a tale had come my way. A ship of His Majesty's Navy had not long come into dock and The Seven Stars was riotously busy that night, our customers shifting around the place, restlessly seeking the best and rowdiest company. But the fellow who beckoned me to his table, alone among them, seemed content to remain seated in one place.

Despite his having chosen the darkest corner of the tavern, I could discern at once that he was not himself a Navy man, for he wore not a uniform, but instead a great and ragged patchwork coat. It was an extraordinary thing, seemingly pieced together from the remnants of a dozen other garments, all of different sizes, colors, and fabrics. The resulting garment was a lumpy, shapeless thing, and yet, I could just discern, held together with the finest and most exquisitely skillful stitching. His collar was turned up, and the wide brim of his ancient leather hat was tilted down toward me. So, now that his beckoning hand had returned to beneath the table, the darkness and his clothing combined to hide from me every last inch of his person save for his dimly visible, unblinking eyes. These I thought to be of different colors, though it was difficult to say for sure in such poor light. I thought it likely that he would be a rough fellow, but in fact when he spoke I found his voice to be soft and refined.

"I wonder, young sir, if you might bring me a plate of stew and a tankard of ale."

"Of course, sir."

"I am indebted to you."

I duly served the strange gentleman his stew and ale and made to leave him, but he bade me stay.

"Please, lad," he said. "Would you grant a sailor a few moments' conversation? I have been long at sea and I would be grateful for a little company."

I joined him gladly for, as I have said, I was weary already from the evening's work. My uncle would no doubt punish me if he saw me but, as usual, he was in the kitchen rather than at the bar, so I reasoned I would be safe.

"Are none of your crew here for company, sir?"

At this he must have smiled a little, for I briefly caught sight of a faint glimmer of dim candlelight on dull teeth in the shadows beneath his hat brim. He twitched a little, too, as if a tiny ripple of laughter had passed through each of the parts of his body in turn.

"Aye, lad," he said. "*Some* of my shipmates are here, right enough. But a soul can spend too long too close to his shipmates. I would rather a little fresh company. Besides, I have a fine tale to tell, if you'll hear it, but it is one that they know very well already."

"A tale? Gladly, sir," I said, though not perhaps with much sincerity, for the weariness in my body infected my voice.

"Ha! You've heard many a yarn from all sorts and all ports, I'll be bound. You must think there's barely a tale of the briny that you've yet to hear. Well, I'll prove you wrong, lad. You have not heard the like of this one, I promise you. For this is a tale of the worst deeds of a dark-hearted scoundrel who betrayed his shipmates: a tale of greed, and of ruthlessness, and of terrible, bloody revenge!"

I had heard similar claims before, and oft enough been disappointed just the same. But I remembered my uncle's words. A sailor likes the shadows to conceal his secrets. Here was a man almost *made* of shadows.

160

Would he not have the darkest secrets to draw upon for his stories? I leaned in toward him, the better to hear his words, and he grinned at my attention.

"There was a ship set sail, some years back—an old tub, her glory days long behind her, but sturdy enough to weather another few squalls yet—sailing to Barbados. It was a smooth enough voyage out. The captain and many of the crew knew the boat and the route well, and the weather and the seas were kind enough, so they arrived in good time and fine spirits. They off-loaded their cargo, and their work, for the moment, was done. So the crew, believing themselves entitled to some rowdy entertainment at the end of a voyage, set about the gaining of sore heads, one way or another, in various taverns around the town.

"When the ship was to set off homeward, three days later, several of the crew had not returned, having been variously waylaid by imprisonment, injury, or amorous entanglements, but the captain deemed that they still had sufficient hands to see them home safe so they did not delay and set sail as planned.

"Now, three days out on the return trip and all's been well so far when something is spotted off the port bow. The captain puts his spyglass to his eye and sees there is a jolly boat, seemingly adrift with no man aboard, but only a gigantic black bear in a cage.

"They sail alongside, expecting that, perhaps, there may be a sailor lying asleep, as yet unseen, who might be able to explain this strange circumstance. But there is none, nor any other clue to aid their understanding. There is only a great black bear, in a cage, in a jolly boat, adrift upon the waters.

"Now this is a rum thing indeed, and sailors may be more prone than most to superstition, as you know, so there is some debate amongst the crew as to what should be done. Some think it an ill omen and best left well alone. Contrarily, others think it will bring them good fortune, so they should bring the beast aboard. And yet others say that superstition can go hang, but surely such a beast could be sold for a good price once they are home. This last argument is the one that finds most favor with the captain, so block and tackle and the strong arms of four sailors hoist the cage aboard, with the bear in it, and the ship continues on her way home.

"Well, the crew are wary of the beast at first: intrigued and fascinated, but also cautious. It is a beautiful creature and black as the devil's shadow, and sailors know enough of dark beauty to be wary of it. But despite its confinement in so small a space this bear proves to be a placid creature, and as the days pass, he grows in the crew's affection. One night, when one sailor plays his squeezebox, the bear rises to his hind legs and dances a crude jig, and this is great entertainment for all. Some of the crew, full of groggy courage, even venture close enough to the cage to push a hand through the bars and stroke that blackest fur, and the bear makes no complaint. It is a happy night for all.

"Well, nearly all. While all else are laughing and carefree, the ship's cook, alone amongst them, has a face like a thunderhead. While ashore, he had spent his time gambling and enjoyed unusual luck. But this night he finds his luck has stayed on land. The cards are against him and he loses all of his winnings and more to the ship's carpenter. There's an angry fire in his belly, which he feeds with an excess of rum. He accuses the carpenter of cheating. There has been bad blood between these two before now, and old wounds sting afresh in the salty air, but the rest of the crew prevent a fight. They know these men of old and they are not alike. The carpenter is a fine fellow, strong and brave and true, but the cook is a sorry soul, selfish and deceitful, a weasel of a man, quite unlike his brother, and—"

"His brother?" I said. The sailor looked up at me, and even with only his eyes discernible in the shadows of his face I thought I read a teasing amusement in his expression.

"Did I not say? The cook and the carpenter are brothers, though two men less alike you would seldom meet. But that's of little matter. Now, where was I? Yes. So the crew keep the men apart and prevent any violence between them and they mock the cook as a poor loser. He swears and fumes and threatens in return, but the crew only laugh harder at his bluster, and eventually he slopes off to his bunk, muttering curses as he goes.

"Well, the drinking and the singing continue awhile in his absence before the captain calls an end to it, takes the night watch himself, and sends his crew to get some sleep.

"The carpenter awakes in his bunk next morning and at once knows something is wrong. There are noises coming from above deck, different ones all at once, that his dozy head cannot quickly disentangle. He rises quickly and sees that others of the crew are doing likewise. There is a good deal of movement on deck. Panicked, heavy feet. And there are shouts and cries, of fear, of pain, and of horror. The carpenter thinks for a moment that they have been boarded by pirates. He goes beneath his bed to take up his knife and there spies that his locker, containing his winnings from the card game, has gone. He curses the cook, presuming him to be the culprit, with harsh words even for a sailor. Anger steels his heart and he climbs the steps to the deck with terrible resolve and without fear. Whatever danger awaits him, he has fury on his side.

"Emerging from the darkness below decks, the light hits the carpenter's eyes, and he is temporarily blinded by the glare of the low sun at the exact moment that he first hears the bear's fearsome roar. His fury turns instantly to terror, and his blindness to darkness, as a huge black shape blocks out the sun. He looks up and the bear is there before him, standing tall and broad and black as the night.

"He idly swings a massive paw and the carpenter is swept aside like a cobweb, though he lands on the deck a deal more heavily. As he rises he takes in the dreadful scene before him. The deck is awash with blood, and strewn with bodies and parts of bodies, dead and dying shipmates, their cries and moans joining in a low murmur of pain. There is the bear's cage, opened. There is the captain slumped dead by the wheel. There is the space where the jolly boat ought to be. There is the bear, raging and roaring as he shrugs off a pistol shot from the brave young cabin boy and repays it with a deadly blow to the head.

"And there, out across the waves beyond the bow rail, is the jolly boat, with the cook rowing it away from the ship, and the carpenter has no doubt that his locker full of coins and jewels is in it, too. The carpenter bellows across the sea to the cook. 'You will die by my hand for this!' he shouts. 'I swear to you, brother: you will die by my hand!' "

At this moment, the sailor raised up his left hand, clenched tight into a fist as if he were grasping on to life itself, and brought it down hard upon the table with a crash. I quite leaped in my seat with surprise, and my companion appeared a little shocked himself, as if startled by his own intemperate action. His right hand, by some instinct, appeared from beneath the table and fell upon the left, covering it, as if trying to conceal its embarrassing violence. Then in an instant, both hands disappeared back beneath the table and the sailor regained his composure. I only glimpsed his hands, so distracted had I been by the thump on the tabletop, and so fleeting was their appearance, but I felt sure that there had been something awry in the way they looked. It seemed they had been as mismatched as his eyes. But I had little time to dwell upon this.

"Then the bear hits the carpenter again!" said the sailor. "And the blow would have killed him had the ship not then rolled on a big swell and knocked the bear off balance. So it's just a glancing blow he receives, and he lands on the deck again with only a broken arm for his troubles and his heart still beating. He ignores the pain and rolls clear of the bear's next lumbering attack, then jumps to his feet and scrambles up the rigging of the mainmast, hoping that the beast cannot follow. In any case he does not, and the carpenter climbs on up (none too quickly with only one good arm) to a fair height, the better to take stock of the situation.

"It is a sorry sight. He can see all of the crew now. They are not all dead, but none are standing, and some have been torn to pieces. The bear is roaming the deck on all fours, roaring wildly. It is a monster now, a raging beast, unrecognizable as the playful pet of the previous evening. The carpenter cannot imagine what can have caused this terrible transformation, but he has no doubt that it is somehow the cook's doing. He casts his eyes out to sea again. The jolly boat is a good distance away now and disappears and reappears as it rides the rolling surface of the waters. The carpenter's good left hand grips the rigging tight, as if it were gripping the cook's neck. And he needs to hold tight, too. He's been up the rigging in far rougher seas than this in the past, and without a care, but with only one good arm, and with no one at the helm to keep the ship steady, it's a fine job he has to do to hold on as the ship pitches and rolls and the mast sways wildly.

"He's wondering what to do next when fate takes a hand in the proceedings. The bear has run over to the bow rail and raised his front paws up onto it, as if he's looking out at that departing wretch the cook, out in the jolly boat. At that moment, a wave strikes the opposite bow and rocks the vessel suddenly over, far enough that the raging bear is sent off balance once again. Then, as a loose barrel rolls fast across the sloping deck and hits him a heavy blow, the bear is tipped clean over the rail with a comical yelp.

"The carpenter hears the splash as the beast hits the water, and then a deal more splashing and yelping and roaring as he surfaces. The next he sees of him, the bear is swimming, already at some distance. He dips and bobs with the waves, which are carrying him away from the ship, and the carpenter watches him awhile, as though he fears the beast may somehow climb back aboard to continue his mayhem. Then he carefully sets about descending to the deck. He is only three steps down toward his goal when there is a dreadful grinding, crunching noise and the ship throws herself sideways as if she wants to shake the carpenter off. For a moment he is hanging from the rigging by his one good hand, his legs dangling over the waves. And, as if this weren't peril enough for a blameless man to suffer, now he spies for the first time the telltale dark fins of prowling sharks."

I confess I had a sudden urge to giggle at this point, and my attempts to mask my amusement with a cough were poorly acted. The sailor stopped his tale and those unnatural eyes fixed me from the dark.

"Do you find my tale amusing, boy?"

He did not blink. I wondered then if he ever did as I could not recall his having done so the whole time he had been talking.

"No, sir," I said. "I was merely startled by the misfortune of this fellow. To encounter a mad bear at sea is most unfortunate in itself. And now sharks. He is surely the most unlucky—"

"Don't," said the sailor in the quietest, firmest voice, "make light of his woes." His burning stare convinced me. I had been smiling, despite my wish to conceal my amusement. I was no longer. After a moment, he went on.

"With no hand at the wheel to steer her, wind and wave have pushed the ship onto a reef, holing her beneath the water. So now here is further misery to amuse you, young sir. For the ship is sinking, and listing to one side as she goes down. The mast to which this poor devil the carpenter is clinging is leaning over ever more severely. He sees the waters lap onto the deck, gradually sweeping them clean of his dead and dying shipmates, sees those bodies—alive and dead—pulled below amidst the thrashing fins and tails of the sharks. He clings on to the rigging in terror as the waters turn crimson and the mast bows down in supplication to those circling demons of the sea.

"He grips his knife and readies himself as he dips into the churning waters. He'll not go out gently, but it is a contest soon ended. The jolly boat is a speck in the distance by now, but the carpenter's eyes are fixed firmly upon it and even as he is dragged below, his mind and heart are full of dark fury at the cook's foul treachery. Then there is darkness. The sharks eat their fill and within minutes all that remains of the entire crew are scraps of men at the bottom of the sea."

"But, sir," said I, "you cannot expect me to think this tale true, for, by your own account, every soul left aboard that ship perished. Only the treacherous cook escaped, and he too early to witness much of what you have related. And besides, you said this was a tale of revenge and yet no one remains to take that revenge."

At this, I caught sight again of a dim scar of a smile within the shadows of the sailor's face.

"You've a keen mind, right enough, lad," he said. "You've reasoned that just beautiful. But there's things as happen at sea that defy reason." He paused for a moment, as if distracted. His eyes flickered just a fraction up and to one side, as if he were looking at

169

something behind me, and his smile widened. I turned to see what possible sight might have amused so dark a soul and saw, on the contrary, only a sight to dismay me: my uncle emerging from behind the bar and striding angrily toward me.

"There's things as defy all explanation," said the sailor. "There's rage that can outlive the mere shell of the body that it inhabits." He began to rise from his seat, and as he did so he raised a hand to that battered leather hat and pulled it forward from his head so that for a moment it obscured his face entirely, but I saw then that across his wrist was a most dreadful scar.

"And if there has not yet been revenge," he said, as his hand dropped to his side and the hat to the floor, "then this tale is not yet ended."

He stepped out from the shadows then and shrugged off that strange patchwork coat, and though the light was still dim, the full horror of his appearance was yet clear enough. He was a big man, but crooked and misshapen, his hulking frame somehow pulled askew. But there was no mistaking the power of him, nor his menace. The shirt he wore was ragged, one sleeve in tatters, the other missing entirely, and so revealed that the scar across his wrist was but one of very many.

These scars crossed and recrossed his arms, dividing up his skin such that it resembled a farmer's fields divided by hedges, each area varying in color and texture, some of them marked by the tattooist's needle. And running along each scar was the same neat stitching as I had noted on his coat. Another such scar arced down over his forehead then ran down beneath his eye and out across the cheek, the skin on either side of the stitching being of different shades. The greater part of that horrible visage was tanned and weather-beaten, but the smaller part confined by the scar was fairer and smoother, the face of a boy. The unholy, mismatched eyes glared with hateful intent and the mouth, all graveyard teeth and torn lips.

I heard my uncle emit an odd small sound behind me, part gasp and part whimper.

"You?" he whispered.

"Aye," said the sailor. His right hand drew a knife from his belt as he lurched forward a step. I pushed back my chair and turned my head again. My uncle was backing away, in a slow, horrific trance, unable to find the will to run, transfixed by fear.

"Did you think you could hide?" said the sailor. He was beside me now and placed his free hand upon my shoulder, a gentle weight to persuade me to stay seated.

"Did you think we would not find you?"

"We? Oh God in heaven!" My uncle's eyes darted over the sailor's body.

"Aye," said the sailor. "The bear and the sharks between them made ugly work of us. But there were scraps enough left by the end still to build from. We have searched for you for so long, driven by burning rage. And now your captain's eye has found you out. And you will die by your brother's hand."

Then the sailor stepped away from me, toward my uncle, and as he did so his left hand, just for an instant, brushed through my hair with a gentle affection that I recognized at once.

Then it took the knife from the right hand, and set to its bloody task.

*M*r. Fowler's story having come to an end, Jack feels disorientated and adrift. The blood-filled narrative had gripped him completely, and for as long as Mr. Fowler had been relating it there had been no one and nothing else in the room. There had only been Mr. Fowler's face, floating in the darkness, the rich music of his voice and the terrible images drawn by his words. Now that it has ended, Jack feels abandoned. His stomach jolts inside him as if he is suddenly falling. It is a terrifying sensation that he tries hard to conceal. He gasps in a desperate breath and holds it, and the panic and the fear subside a little, his racing heart slows. He keeps his unblinking eyes set on Mr. Fowler's, and he smiles.

Mr. Fowler smiles back. "I hope that passed muster," says Mr. Fowler.

"Oh, it did, Mr. Fowler," says Frances, her voice full of admiration, and even silent Mr. Randolph gives a subtle nod of approval.

Jack nods, too, though it was more than just the story itself that scared him; it was Mr. Fowler himself. Jack looks at him now. Rivers of shadow run along the cavernous lines of his face, widening and narrowing as the candlelight flickers, drawing and redrawing his features, as if he is one man with myriad faces. All of those faces smiling, though. And it is a kindly smile, almost enough to reassure.

"Thank you, Mr. Fowler. If you please . . ." says Mr. Osterley.

173

With his eyes still on Jack, Mr. Fowler leans forward. As he does so, the light hits his face at such an angle that, just for a second, his kindly smile is transformed into a sinister leer. Then he blows out the flame, pushes back his chair, and all but disappears into the darkness.

It was only a trick of the light, Jack knows, but that snapshot moment was another crumb to feed that worm of doubt in his head, to make him reconsider what is possible, and what impossible, in the world. And he thinks again about the marks on Frances Crane's wrists, and the worm writhes and turns and grows.

Just four flames left now, and the table is like a boat of light in a sea of darkness. The room has almost ceased to exist, and those who have already told their stories are just dim shapes in the gloom.

"Miss Crane," says Mr. Osterley. "If you'd be so kind."

Frances smiles at him, all traces of her recent distress now utterly vanished. "Of course," she says, then addresses everyone else, in light or in darkness. "I think you'll like my story tonight. Most of you anyway. Some of you already know I was a painter, before. I used to have a lot of friends who were artists of one kind or another: painters and sculptors and dancers and singers and musicians and writers and poets.

"This story is one that one of the writers once told me: not one he wrote, just one he'd heard somewhere.

He was a good writer, for a while at least, but he was always worried that he might run out of ideas. Said he hated that question that writers always get asked: 'Where do you get your ideas from?' Because he didn't know the answer, and that scared him. Anyway, because of that, I think, he was always very taken by this story. He told it to me a few times, actually. I think he told it a lot, and forgot who had already heard it, and I could never bring myself to tell him. But at least that means I can remember it well."

Unputdownable

J ames was lost. He'd suspected as much for some time, but now he was sure. The man at the garage just outside town had given him directions, but James hadn't written them down and now he'd forgotten most of them. He pulled the car into the parking lot by the library, just so he could stop and have a think. What he thought was that a library was probably a pretty good place to get some help. He got out of the car, stretched, and went in.

The library was a decent size, especially for so small a town, and well stocked with books, albeit mostly rather old ones. The carpet looked a few years past its best, too. There was no one at the desk at the moment—in fact, there seemed to be no one else there at all—so he wandered around the shelves for a while, occasionally picking up a book at random and pretending to look at it while keeping half an eye out for a member of the staff, but there was still nobody in sight.

"Are you looking for anything in particular?"

James squeaked slightly as he jumped in surprise, then spun around to see a small young woman with an unusually tall hairdo looking up at him with a smile. She had a badge pinned to her sweater that said *Senior Library Assistant* in printed letters and then *Mary* handwritten with a black marker pen beneath. Where had she come from? And were all librarians so quiet? Did they get some kind of special ninja librarian training?

"Sorry. What?" said James.

"I said: Are you looking for anything in particular?"

"Actually, yes," said James. "I'm looking for my home."

The girl thought about this for a moment, still smiling. "Well," she said, pointing to the nearest shelf, "I'm pretty sure you won't find it in zoology. Not unless you're a snail, anyway. But then, a snail wouldn't ever lose his home, would he?"

She had a good smile, warm and mischievous at once, but James was too tired to fully appreciate it, or her joking tone. In return he only looked bemused.

"Sorry," said the girl. "You're looking for your home. How do you mean? And how can I help?"

"I'm moving into my new place today. I rented a house near here—at least, I *hope* it's near here—only I got a bit lost. I've been driving around for ages. I spent quite a while wondering why a town as small as this had two libraries. And then when I saw the third one, and it looked exactly the same as the other two, I finally realized I was going around in circles. So I thought I'd stop and ask for some help." He made a helpless face. "Help?"

"Yup," said Mary the assistant librarian. "That one-way system doesn't let go easily, does it? You know, my theory is that half the population of the town never actually meant to live here; they just came to do some shopping and never got out. Shall I draw you a map?"

"That'd be great. I got some directions from the guy at the garage up the road there, but I forgot most of them. He called it The Writer's House. You don't know anything about that, do you?"

"Afraid not, no."

So James told her the address of the house and Mary found a road atlas and drew him a map. While she did, James browsed through the old books on a cart by the desk, marked *Book Sale. Withdrawn from stock.* James picked one out almost at random, a thick, battered paperback priced in pencil on the first page at 25 pence. It wasn't the kind of thing he'd usually buy, but he took it anyway, paying with a handful of change as Mary handed him the map.

It wasn't far, and when he got there, it didn't take long to unpack. James had brought everything he owned in the world with him, and found that it had fitted all too easily into the trunk and backseat of his car. And it wasn't a big car.

His life had gone a bit wrong lately, but this was to be his fresh start. He arranged his few possessions in their appropriate rooms while listening to music he didn't like on his radio. The house felt empty and unfamiliar, but then, he reasoned, it *was* empty and unfamiliar.

When he was done, he made a mug of tea and sat on his bed to read for a while. He wasn't usually much of a reader (it was odd that he'd bought the book at all), but for the time being he had no television, so he plowed through the first few chapters. It was diverting enough, just a cheap thriller: dumb and action-packed, like the movies he usually watched. In any case, he liked it enough to keep reading. In fact, it was odd but, while he knew it wasn't very good, really, he found— for the first time in his life—that he just wanted to carry on and on reading it.

He had never understood before when someone called a book "unputdownable," but here he was frantically turning the pages, drinking in every badly written word, devouring the pages like a starved man, reading much faster than he'd even known he was able to. He read on, longer than he'd intended, only rather briefly (and reluctantly) stopping to make and eat some supper. Then, with nothing pressing to occupy him after his meal, he decided he might as well continue. He raced through a few chapters in the armchair in the living room and then, when he started to feel chilly, he took the book to bed, intending to read just one more chapter before going to sleep.

He finished it at three thirty-five in the morning. He was puzzled that he'd needed so badly to get to the end, but by then he was too exhausted to really think too much about it. He slept deeply and solidly, but only until a little after dawn. Almost immediately on waking he started to think about the book again. He hadn't liked the ending. His guess at who had committed the murder had been wrong, and he'd been disappointed by that. Only now he thought that it wasn't he that was wrong: his was the right ending; the author of the book had got it wrong.

He got out of bed just long enough to find a pen, then he got back in and turned to the back of the book. There were half a dozen blank pages right at the back, and with his cheap ballpoint pen, he started to write on these, in tiny, densely packed letters. Just for fun he wrote down his own ending to the story.

James was surprised to find that it came to him easily; it felt as if he wasn't even thinking about it. As if he wasn't thinking of the words and *then* writing them down, but instead he was writing them down and then reading them. He was amazed and delighted by himself. He hadn't ever thought of himself as having a good imagination, or that he could write particularly well, and yet here he was pouring words onto a page (onto several pages) with the same determination with which he had read the book the previous night. He finished at the very end of the last page—a perfect fit—and sat back in the bed, slightly breathless, elated and startled.

He flicked through the pages. There were no mistakes, no crossings out, no corrections. He read the occasional sentence here and there as he glanced through. It seemed to be good. Better, he thought, than the writing in the book itself.

"Well, where did that come from?" he said to himself aloud. He stared at his hand accusingly. The pen had leaked some ink onto his fingertips and now the hand almost didn't feel or look like it belonged to him. It was all very odd, but he guessed that he was just a bit disoriented by the move and a general feeling of not yet belonging. A huge yawn took hold of him and pushed such thoughts away.

"Breakfast," he said, and got up and had some.

After breakfast, James drove to town. He went to a supermarket full of harsh light and chirpy music and bought a number of things he needed for the house. He had written a list earlier and then left it on the kitchen table when he went out, but he was pretty sure he had remembered everything. He also got a few things that hadn't been on the list but that suddenly seemed necessary once he saw them on the shelves. Then he made an excellent job of finding his way home again, only passing the library twice this time.

Back home, he swore at himself briefly once he found his shopping list and realized all the things he'd forgotten, then he set about finding places for all that he had bought: this cupboard for plates and dishes, this one for cups and glasses, this one for jars and tins, and so on. There was little enough that it didn't take him long.

A couple of the items that he had bought on impulse he left out on the kitchen table: a packet of six notebooks and a pack of a dozen cheap ballpoint pens. James sat at the table and stared at these. He couldn't remember why he'd bought them, but thinking back he remembered he'd felt a small thrill as he placed them in his cart. Stupid, really. Oh well, now that he had them, the notebooks might as well be of some use, he thought.

He tore open the plastic wrapping and took one out. He needed to be more organized from now on, he told himself, so he decided to write a proper shopping list for tomorrow, and a list of things he needed to do. He took a pen from the box and removed the cap.

But he didn't write a list because, as he folded back the cover of the book and looked at the empty page of lined paper beneath, a thought occurred to him. He found he was thinking about a child he had seen sitting on a low wall outside the supermarket: a girl, maybe twelve years old. She looked as if she needed to cry but wasn't going to let herself. She was holding her lips tight together, looking first off to one side and then the other, as if trying to shake off the attention of anyone who might look at her. James had wondered what her story was.

And then, because he couldn't know, he made one up.

It was almost dark, and he was hungry and his hand hurt. He felt as if he had just woken up, but he wasn't in bed: he was sitting at the kitchen table. He got up and switched the light on, feeling woozy and unsettled, stretched his arms out and his head back, trying to work the tension out of his muscles. He wished he could do the same for the tension inside his head.

Then he looked down at the kitchen table and saw the notebook. It was open at a page about two-thirds of the way through, a page covered in writing. When he picked up the book and looked through it, he found that all the pages before that were the same. It was his handwriting, but he had no memory of writing it. James dropped the book onto the table in shock, backing away from it as if afraid. Was he going mad? When he had calmed down a little, he made a cup of tea, glancing at the book suspiciously out of the corner of his eye as he did so. Then he sat, picked up the book gingerly, swallowed hard, and began to read.

It was really good.

At least, he was fairly certain it was good. It was much better than James could ever believe he was capable of writing, that was for sure. But there it was, in his handwriting, and as he read it there was a dim ring of familiarity to it, as if he'd at least *read* the story before. But how could he have written it? He didn't write. He couldn't even *tell* stories very well, much less write them. But here was the story of the crying girl, richly imagined and set out in precise detail, beautifully and touchingly written.

It was amazing. Frightening, too.

He remembered a story he had heard on the news once. There had been a man who had been hit on the head and had suddenly found that he could play the piano rather brilliantly, despite never having done so at all previously. James wondered if the same thing could happen with writing. And without being hit on the head. The whole thing seemed crazy. Luckily, his hunger helped distract him, and he set aside the book to make himself some cheese on toast.

He wolfed it down, in that way that you can when you're on your own and nobody's watching. Then he made more and did it again. At the end of it he felt full, sated, fulfilled. Elated, in fact. And not at all tired. He couldn't decide what to do next, but *anything* seemed possible.

Ten minutes later he was fast asleep, fully clothed, on his bed.

When he awoke, late the next morning, he felt amazing. There was an energy in him like he had never known before, and a feeling of deep satisfaction. He sang to himself as he made a huge bowl of porridge for his breakfast, far too much for only one person. Then, when he had eaten it all, he had two pieces of thickly cut toast, generously buttered and laden with jam, all of it washed down with mugs of tea. And it all tasted incredible, like the best porridge, the best toast, the best jam, and the best tea ever made. He felt incredibly alive, his skin singing, his mind happily racing.

He looked at the notebook, half expecting it to be empty, to discover he had dreamed the whole thing.

Or else it would be full of gibberish. But no; it was as he remembered it, still (so far as he could judge) very good, maybe even brilliant. This morning he found it easier to just accept it, somehow. And he had other things on his mind, too. He had decided to look for a job, just temporarily. He had enough money put aside that he could get by for a while, but he wanted something to do, to keep his mind and body occupied.

Another trip to town, to the Job Center, was called for, so he showered and dressed and drove off in his complaining heap of a car.

He hadn't planned to go to the library, but the parking lot beside it was convenient, and while he was there he thought he might as well. The same girl, Mary, was behind the desk, filing buff-colored record cards. She looked up at the sound of the door opening.

"Oh, hello again, Lost Boy. Did you find your way home, then?"

"Um, yes, thanks."

"And now that you're living in the neighborhood, I suppose you figured you'd join the library, like all solid upstanding citizens should?"

"Um, yes," said James. Actually, the thought hadn't occurred to him even for a moment. He hadn't ever joined a library in his life—why would he? But now, somehow, the idea appealed. "What do I need to—"

"Here you go." Mary plucked a photocopied sheet of paper from a plastic holder on the front of the

188

counter and offered it to him with a theatrical flourish. "Just fill in this form, bring us some ID and proof of address, and that's pretty much it. I'd take you through it in detail, but it's all pretty self-explanatory, unless you're some kind of idiot. And you want to join the library, so you're clearly not."

James glanced down at the form. "Well, I don't know about that," he said. "But I think I'll manage. Thanks. I'll, uh, see you in a day or two." He made for the door and Mary waved him a distracted good-bye as she returned her attention to her record cards.

"See you later, navigator," she said.

James didn't get home until early evening in the end. After a fruitless visit to the employment agency, and then a large, unhealthy, hugely enjoyable lunch in a café, he made a spontaneous trip to the movie theater and accidentally saw the beginning and end (he slept soundly through the middle) of a black-and-white German film.

While he had been out, the story he had written hadn't even crossed his mind, but now that he was home, he found himself thinking about it again. The notebook was on the kitchen table, open at the final page of writing. He thought he would read through it one more time.

But when he sat down, instead of turning back to the start of the book, he unthinkingly turned over to a blank page. Why had he done that? he wondered. And then he noticed that he had picked up the pen, too, which was odd as he had no intention of writing anything. He had barely a thought in his head, after all.

Or he hadn't. Now, actually, there *was* something, or the beginning of something, at least . . .

His hand hurt again, but it took some time to notice because his head hurt so much more. Something else was wrong, too, if only he could work out what it was. Perhaps if it wasn't so dark it would be easier. He wondered why his cheek felt so odd.

Ah yes, he was lying on the kitchen floor. That was it. One of his legs was tangled up in his chair, though he didn't realize this until he tried (and failed) to stand up. Now his knee hurt, too. He freed his leg from the toppled chair and carefully raised himself to his feet to take stock of the situation. He supposed he must have fallen asleep at the table and fallen off his chair. He touched a hand to his head and discovered that this was a very effective way of being in yet more pain. He stumbled about until he found the light switch, then made his way up to the bathroom to stand in front of the mirror and survey the damage.

He wasn't bleeding. That was good. But his cheek was very red and he suspected that he'd gain a pretty respectable bump on his head by the morning. He parted his hair at the site of the pain and tried to take a look in the mirror, but he couldn't really see. He was reminded again, though, of the stiffness and pain in his fingers. He took a look at his right hand, turning it and flexing the fingers. The discomfort was freshly familiar, jolting his memory. He'd been writing again, he could vaguely recall. But what, he had no idea.

He had finished the first notebook and continued into the second, almost filling that, too. It was, he thought, an extraordinary amount of words to have written in one night, even if he had been just copying them from a book. To have also composed them from scratch (and again, written them out in a neat, compact hand without a single correction) in that time defied belief.

The pages rustled and flapped in his shaking hands as he flicked through them. He felt panicked and short of breath. What was happening to him? Where were they coming from, all these words? He put the books down, paced around the room for a while, his mind full of fast-moving nothingness. After some minutes he got his thoughts to settle, then he braced himself and sat down to read.

The thing that scared him most was not that this story was more brilliant than the last (though even he could see that it was), nor that it seemed only faintly familiar to him, even though he had apparently been the one to write it, nor even that the content of the story was so dark and twisted. What worried him was a single word on the penultimate page: *quotidian*.

He had no idea what it meant. He had never heard it before, much less ever used it. Was it even a real word? He had no idea. But *he* had written it, apparently. Or at least his hand had held the pen that had written it. His steady hand. Not this one that was quivering before him now.

Mary wasn't used to having customers waiting outside the library door for her to open up in the morning.

"You're keen," she said, but James rushed by her without a word, heading straight for the reference section. "Suit yourself," she muttered.

Quotidian really was a word. What's more, it was a word he had used perfectly correctly in a short work of fiction that, by any reasonable judgment, it was fair to say he was in no way capable of having written.

"Have you filled in your form, then?" said the girl when he went unsteadily over to the desk.

"No. Um . . ." He fumbled in his pocket and found the form, looked at it with dazed puzzlement. "Um, yes. Yes, I have." He had indeed filled in the application form; it was just that he had no memory of doing so. He handed it over, then his driving license and a letter from the electric company.

The girl nodded, filled in a form of her own, and told him, a little brusquely, that he'd have his card in a few days.

James did not respond. He looked confused, a little lost. The girl was still trying to weigh whether to ask him what was wrong, or tell him to leave, when a short, stout man wearing a ratty jacket and a flat cap, and in his sixties came in. He looked at James with wide eyes, overacting surprise.

"Blimey, Mary. Two people in here at once? Haven't seen that since the fifties. I hope they'll be giving you some extra staff to cope."

"Morning, George," said the girl, smiling and handing him a copy of the *Financial Times*. "Enjoy your crossword." He shuffled off toward one of the tables. James hadn't moved. "Was there anything else?" she asked him.

"Eh? Sorry. I, uh . . . I didn't sleep too well last night. Look, um . . . this is going to sound crazy, but . . ." He was looking to one side of her, avoiding meeting her eyes. One of his fingers was tapping erratically on top of a pair of notebooks he had put down on her desk. The last time she'd seen anyone so nervous in her company the man in question had proposed marriage (without success). "Um, look . . . do you . . ." He shook his head, as if trying to rattle his thoughts into some sort of order. "Do you know how I could find out about who used to live in my house? In The Writer's House? How could I find out who the writer was?"

"Well, I suppose—" Mary began.

"French fella," said George, without looking up from his crossword. "I think French. Foreign anyway. Before my time here, but I heard all about him. Young chap. Locked himself away in that place, scribbling away. Wrote two books, then went mad."

193

James's face crumpled. "Mad?"

"Well, he killed himself anyway. Got to be a bit mad to do that, haven't you? Funny lot those arty-crafty types, aren't they? Highly strung. Why d'you ask, though?"

But James was already halfway out the door.

Mary thought more than twice about whether to go to the house. She had the address from James's application form, but she figured that he'd probably be back once he realized that he'd left his notebooks behind. She also realized she could quite easily mail the books back to him if that was her real concern.

But after two weeks she still hadn't. She'd read them in the meantime, though, several times over. She'd meant just to take a glance, kidding herself that she was checking in case James had written a phone number inside somewhere, but of course once she'd read the beginning she couldn't stop herself.

She'd found out who The Writer's House had belonged to as well. She'd asked a few of her regulars until a half-remembered title gave her enough of a lead to find his name. Then, out of interest, she'd tracked down copies of both his novels in other branches and had them transferred over.

When she read them she recognized the style at once.

The second book to arrive had been published after his death. It was a dark and disturbing story, but it was the "about the author" page that finally shocked her into action.

She drove to the house straight after work. There was no answer to her knock, but the door wasn't locked when she tried it.

She was sure, as soon as she saw him, that James was dead. She stood in the doorway for a long moment, staring at the scene before her, shocked into a strange numbness. It was horrible but fascinating.

Perhaps because of the chaos around it, it was the neat pile of notebooks that held her attention. There was a reassuring normalness to them, order and familiarity (they were the same kind of books Mary had used at school). They looked like something from real life. So she focused on the books, and chose not to dwell on any of the rest of it for now. In a daze, she shuffled over to the table and picked up the books. They were numbered on their covers from three to six. As a librarian, and a respecter of the correct order of things, she dutifully opened up book three and, on an impulse, began to read.

By the time she had finished book six, it was the early hours of the morning. She slept briefly before she continued to read, slowly finding some order in the rest of James's final writings: on loose sheets of paper, the backs of envelopes, paper towels, and elsewhere. James's handwriting had deteriorated as he went along and this helped her to find the correct order, and told her at once that the writing on the table itself (still reasonably legible) preceded the less-controlled writing on the walls, and that the wild scrawl on James's own left arm came last.

She had expected an ending. She had, in fact, relied upon it. She had had to steel herself to read (with difficulty) the last words trailed over James's pale, dead skin, had known she should have stopped long ago, should not even have started. But the writing—the beautiful, elegant, seductive sentences—had compelled her to go on. Now that they had run out she felt sick, twice over: once from gorging herself, and once for still feeling unsatisfied.

There had to be an ending.

She searched the room frantically for some other, previously overlooked scrap of paper that might contain it, checked every surface, ran through the rest of the house in case it might have been set down in some other room.

At last she was forced to conclude that there simply was no ending. James had written himself to death, but whatever madness had forced him to do so, had kept him from sleeping or eating for days, had drained all these words and his life from him, had still not completed its task.

Back in the kitchen, dawn's light breaking through the window, Mary sank, exhausted, to the floor. She glanced resentfully at James's body sprawled across the tabletop and then, appalled at this reaction, shook herself into recognizing the awfulness of what she had done. What had she been thinking? She would go now, return to town, and telephone the police. Or should she call for an ambulance? She wasn't sure. But she would go and belatedly do what was needed. She couldn't believe how the writing had gripped her, nor how overwhelmingly she had felt the need for an ending to the story.

Well, there could never be one now, so there was no point thinking about it.

Unless . . .

A thought occurred to her. She had a notebook and a pen in her pocket. And there was a larger notepad in the car if she needed it. She was already onto the second page of the notebook, her writing dense and neat and flowing quickly.

James and the world fell away, and all that was left were words.

*F*rances Crane sits still for a moment. She is leaning
forward, propped up on one arm. Her head is
bowed. She looks drained, as if the telling of her story
has sapped all the energy from her, wiped away her
playful smile.

"Are you okay?" says Jack.

Frances looks up at him. "Yes," she says hesitantly.
"Yes, thank you." She throws him a cursory smile. A
weak little thing that dies in a second. "That one affects
me more than most for some reason, but I always
forget. Maybe it's because it reminds me of what
happened to my writer friend."

"What was that?"

"In the end he did run out of ideas. Suddenly
couldn't write anything more. And then, well, then I'm
afraid he killed himself. And nobody saw it coming,
because he always seemed so happy. That's so often the
way, though, isn't it? Nobody sees." Then she manages
another smile—a narrow, flat kind of a thing—before
she blows out her candle and backs away into the thick-
ening darkness.

"Thank you," says Mr. Osterley.

Three flames left now: Mr. Osterley's, Mr. Randolph's,
and Jack's, and the candles are burning low.

It doesn't surprise Jack when Mr. Osterley calls
upon Mr. Randolph to take the next turn. He had
begun to suspect that this strange ritual must end with
Jack and Mr. Osterley facing each other alone in the

*light. But nor is he relieved. Because Jack is beginning
to realize what his story must be when his turn comes.
And while he is scared to tell it, he will not run, because
the other story—the story of this night of stories—is
not yet over. And he wants to know how that story ends.*

But first there will be Mr. Randolph's turn.

"This is my own story," says Mr. Randolph.

*He closes his eyes for a moment, and when he opens
them again it seems to Jack that he has taken himself
away somewhere, to another time and another place.
And just for a moment there is a trace of a smile on that
cold face of his.*

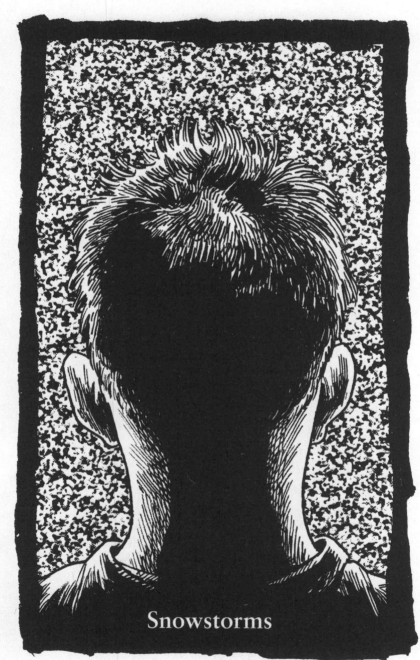

Snowstorms

Jenny, my sister, gave me a snowstorm. You know, those toys with a scene in a glass globe full of water, and when you shake it up it snows? One of those. Got it for me as a parting gift, when she heard that I was going to the Antarctic for six months.

Pretty good joke.

She made another joke, too. She said: "It's a long way to go just because you're scared of the dark." Because I had been, a bit, when we were kids, and because when I got to Oates—the Captain Oates Research Station—in October, the sun would have just come up. And it wouldn't be going down again until March. That's how it is there: a day that lasts half a year. They warned me about it at the job interview. Apparently, it sends some people a bit crazy, but I wasn't worried.

Didn't think I'd mind being there with so few people, either. Never been what you'd call sociable. Thought being in a remote place with only a dozen other people would suit me. Thirteen of us. But even with only a small crew, there can still be someone who'll drive you mad. Drive *me* mad, at least. Most of them did a bit, from time to time, I suppose. But the worst of them was Jim Bailey. Bloody Jim Bailey. Jim Bailey, who thought he was funny, but wasn't.

203

He thought he was funny because he was always telling jokes. Didn't bother him that he only knew three. Didn't notice that no one ever laughed.

These were his "jokes":

Whenever anybody left the station he'd say, "Better wrap up warm. It's cold out."

Whenever he got anyone a drink he'd say, "Do you want ice with that?" Even if it was tea or coffee.

Whenever he went outside he'd say, "I may be some time." Only, unlike Captain Oates, he always came back.

At least, for the first five weeks he did.

Then one morning he went out on one of the ski-doos (the snowmobiles we used) on his own. You're not meant to do that. It's stupid. It was especially stupid for Jim Bailey because he rode a ski-doo like a maniac. And it was particularly stupid just then because our radios had been down for a couple of days. Some kind of atmospheric thing, we thought. At least, Deeta—our radio geek—couldn't find anything wrong with the sets themselves, so we assumed it had to be that. Couldn't contact the other bases, couldn't talk to Jim Bailey out on his own on a ski-doo and ask him what the hell he thought he was doing.

And this time he really *was* quite some time. Long enough that something must have happened. Long enough that he'd either broken down or crashed. And I knew he hadn't broken down because I was the one who looked after the ski-doos, and I was good at my job.

But then a crash wasn't likely, either, because there isn't really anything to crash into out there. But this was Jim Bailey. If anyone could find a way of crashing in the middle of a big, flat expanse of featureless ice with nothing to be seen in any direction for miles, then it was him.

And if he had crashed, or broken down somehow, then most likely he was dead. Because Oates was the newest and southernmost of the UK Antarctic Survey's bases, and we were too far away from any of the others, or the nearest US base, to reach them. But there were a few derelict facilities dotted around the area. So it was just possible that Bailey might have found his way to some hut half buried in the snow since the seventies or something. And if he'd done that, then it was just possible he might still be alive.

So we had to go and look for him. And as the radios were out of action, it was decided that the guy who could fix the ski-doos had better be part of the search party.

I was not happy.

There were three remaining ski-doos, so two others from the crew went out with me: Ambler and Cole. They were all right, that pair. Knew each other from working together at another base before. Cole was a big fella, and funny. Used to sing to himself without realizing he was doing it.

Used to.

Ambler was a scrawny-looking sort of bloke, and a bit of a worrier. Only ever seemed to have time for his work and nothing much else. But, like I say, he was all right. Anyway, we wrapped up warm and we set off. The rest of the crew saw us off. Or at least they stood about watching us go out the door, but nobody said very much. I don't think anyone expected it to go well.

At least we had a trail to follow. Deeta had seen which way Bailey had headed off, and no one else had gone that way lately, so there was a clear set of tracks. And, it being the summer after all, the weather wasn't so bad: it was only −40°F, and visibility was good. It wasn't snowing, but that's rare anyway. Apparently, technically speaking, it's a desert out there: it's all about the amount of precipitation, nothing to do with heat. Jim Bailey told me that, I think—it's certainly the kind of thing he would say.

Half an hour out from the base and we realized we didn't need to follow the tracks anymore. Ambler saw it first: Bailey's ski-doo, abandoned. At first glance there was no obvious damage to it. Close-up it was just the same. I tried the engine and it started the first time, as I'd expected. There was nothing wrong with it, not a mark on it. The engine just purred beautifully, until I turned it off.

We took a look around. We were on a flat, feature-less plain of blue-white ice, with good visibility in all directions, a clear view right to the horizon, and we were looking for a man in a bright red coat. If he'd been there, you'd have to figure we'd've spotted him.

But there was no sign.

"Who leaves a perfectly good ski-doo and decides he'd rather walk in this place?" Cole said.

"An idiot," I said.

"Uh-huh. Okay," said Cole. "But which way did the idiot go?"

"Are we near anything here?" I said.

"There was an outpost . . ." Ambler was looking at a map and a compass and slowly turning himself around on the spot. Then he stopped turning and looked up, out across the big white nothing, frowning. "About three miles that way." He pointed. "Finnish geophysicists back in the seventies. But it's likely buried by now, and I doubt Bailey even knew it was there."

"No," I said. "But it's the place we should look."

"Why?"

"Because if he's anywhere else then he's dead anyway."

There was no wind. No sound except our breathing and the crunch of the ice beneath our feet as we shuffled and shifted our weight from side to side. Keeping warm, or nervous; I'm not sure which.

Ambler nodded. "OK. Let's go."

It took us about fifteen minutes on the ski-doos to get to the right spot, then fifteen more before Cole spotted the nearly buried outpost. The entrance was just visible above the surface of the ice, a slit of darkness gaping up from the whiteness, like the mouth of a drowning man gasping for air. We parked up and looked in.

The snow had piled up, forming a natural ramp up to a mailbox-sized gap into the small domed building. No answer when we shouted in, and no footprints leading up to the entrance, so we knew there couldn't be anyone in there. But we decided that one of us had to go in anyway. And Cole and Ambler knew each other from before, so I got outvoted.

I scrambled up the slope, and had to crawl through the gap on my belly because it was so narrow. While I was trying to squeeze through, Cole started giggling, watching me struggling and flailing about, and that set Ambler off, too. Don't think I'd ever heard him laugh before. Just a nervous reaction, I suppose, but it made me angry at the time. I was just about to shout at them to shut up when I finally managed to haul myself through, and dropped.

The snow sloped down sharply inside, so I slid down hard and fast, yelling out in surprise and setting the other two laughing even harder. I came to a standstill with a mouthful of snow, my cheeks burning with cold and embarrassment. I could hear the other two laughing outside. I shouted and swore at them to shut up, but the angrier I got, the harder they laughed. And the harder they laughed, the angrier I got, so eventually I decided to ignore them and get on.

There was hardly any light getting through but it was still enough to see that there was nothing and no one there. It was a tiny space and the Finnish team had done a thorough job of clearing it out. I turned the flashlight on anyway and kicked around in the snow on the floor for a while just because, well, we'd gone a long way to get there and it just seemed right to take the time. But there really was nothing.

I realized as I moved to make my way back out that Ambler and Cole had stopped laughing, but then the silence was broken by another noise.

A dull thump, then a quiet cry. Then a moment of muffled conversation that I couldn't make out.

I shouted, "All right out there?" No reply.

I made my way out again, lumbering up the slope, cursing, and posted myself back out into the light. The glare off the ice did my eyes in for a second. Everything was nothing. Then when I could see again, I realized that Ambler and Cole were gone.

I trudged down the ice slope to where they'd been standing, shouted out their names. No answer. And there were three small splashes of blood on the ice.

Then I saw the footprints leading off around the shelter. Well-spaced, long strides—Ambler and Cole moving quickly. And another drop of blood every other footstep. Once I was around the dome I could see them, orange specks on the snow at the end of a line of footprints, too far off to hear me shouting. They were walking away from me, Cole ahead, walking really purposefully, Ambler behind, waving his arms about as if he was trying to get him to stop. If I'd been thinking straight I'd have gotten on a ski-doo to go after them, but instead I ran. Well, not much of a run. The clothing you wear in those parts isn't exactly built for speed. But I took long strides and swung my arms, like a child pretending to be a giant, or an astronaut bounding about on the moon.

By the time I caught up with them, Ambler was in front of Cole, facing him, bracing himself, ready to physically block his path. He was barely half Cole's size so he'd've struggled to manage it, but Cole had come to a halt anyway. He was hunched over, like the air was leaking out of him, and he was staring up at Ambler, looking dazed, like he'd just woken up and didn't know where he was. Took a while before anyone said anything.

"He thought he saw someone," Ambler said to me. He had a thin, bloody, snotty icicle trailing down from one nostril over his beard.

"Bailey?" I said.

Cole said, "No." He was staring off into the distance, squinting in confusion, and then wide-eyed and surprised. Then he blinked once and turned his head my way, looked me straight in the eyes.

"It was a boy," he said.

I looked at him very closely. I didn't know what to say. It couldn't have been a boy. And Cole must have known that.

"I know it doesn't make any sense," he said, clear and calm, and still looking me straight in the eye. "I know it can't have been. But it *was*. It was a boy. Maybe . . . twelve, thirteen years old."

I turned my head, looking off over the white expanse in all directions. Obviously there was no boy. And there was nowhere for a boy to be and not be seen. But I didn't say anything.

He said: "I know. I do know."

I glanced at Ambler and he shrugged back at me, overacting it so that the gesture was still clear even through the thick padding of his coat.

I pointed at the messy frozen blood in his moustache and beard. "What happened?"

He said: "Cole bumped into me when he set off after this boy he says he saw. Kind of headbutted me by accident."

"So he's had a bang on the head?"

"No," said Cole. "Well, yes, a bit. But *after* I saw the boy. It wasn't a concussion, if that's what you're thinking." He scowled. "I just . . . saw something impossible . . . that no one else did, that's all."

We all stood there for a minute. Ambler wiped the back of his glove under his nose and most of the icy, bloody snot there broke off and fell to the ground.

I said: "Let's get back."

And they didn't take any persuading. We walked back to the ski-doos, along the trail of our footprints. And there *were* only *our* footprints.

The cold had gotten into us by the time we got back to the base. We trudged up the steps in silence. I was thinking about Bailey. Feeling sad about him, but not *only* sad, because I really hadn't liked him. So I also felt guilty about the fact that he was almost certainly dead. As if it was my fault somehow. And I was wondering how the others would take it, too.

At the top of the steps, the door was open.

Cole was at the front. He shouted in: "Hey! Who left the door open? Were you all born in a barn?" He was trying to be funny, trying to sound like his old self, but he didn't.

There was no answer. Everyone was gone.

We looked really carefully to make sure—especially once we realized that all the cold-weather gear was still there—but there really weren't very many places to look. Everyone was gone. And they hadn't wrapped up warm before they went.

We ended up in the rec room. When we spoke, our breath made ghosts in the air.

Cole said: "What's happening? What happened?" There was no point answering. We'd all run through the same thoughts. Everyone was gone. Everyone had gone outside, on foot, without cold-weather gear. For no reason. There was no sign of anything bad having happened, no sign of a struggle, nothing to suggest they were forced to leave—not that there was anyone for miles around anyway. They just went out. It made no sense.

I realized Ambler was speaking to me. "Do you want some?"

"What?"

"I said I'm going to make some tea. Do you want some?"

Tea. Ridiculous. Normal.

"Yes, please," I said, and Cole grunted and nodded. We all shambled into the mess. No one said anything as the kettle boiled, the switch flicked itself off, and Ambler poured the steaming water into the mugs. We waited, silent and staring, while the tea brewed, the room still cold from the door being open. Then Ambler stirred sugar into Cole's tea, and the tinkling of the teaspoon on the mug rang out bell-like in the silence. Cole and I glanced a thank you at him as he handed us our mugs, and it was the first time we'd looked him in the eye in minutes. Then we stood around, warming our hands around the hot mugs, but none of us drinking.

Ambler said: "Shouldn't we go out and look for them?"

Of course we should. It was the obvious thing. But somehow it was equally obvious that there was no use. We could feel they were gone. We wouldn't find them. Nor any trace of them.

I looked at Cole. "Tell me about the boy," I said.

He looked at me, startled. No, wait, not *startled*. *Embarrassed*, maybe.

"There was no boy. Can't have been, can there? I imagined . . . must have . . ." He rubbed a palm against the side of his head, squinting and scowling. "I haven't been sleeping well lately. I don't think—"

"What did you see, Paul?" said Ambler softly, touching a fingertip to Cole's shoulder, like he was just very gently adjusting his balance, steadying him.

Cole looked down at the floor, breathing very deliberately, as if he was concentrating on it: in and out, in and out. Then he looked up at Ambler, eyes wide as saucers. He said: "He was about twelve, I should think. It was hard to tell at that distance, but I think so. Blond hair—" Then he shook his head. "That can't be right, can it? Bareheaded out there. And his clothes . . ."

"What?"

"Well, he was dressed for winter back home. Not here. He had, like, a short overcoat on. And a scarf." He was frowning now. Remembering, but not happy with what he was remembering. "I think he was wearing rain boots."

"Rain boots?" said Ambler. "Here?"

"I know," said Cole, and his voice was crumbling now, breaking apart. "I think, maybe . . ." He looked at Ambler. He said: "Am I going mad?"

"This boy," I said to Ambler. "Did *you* see anything?"

"No." He nodded at Cole. "He ran past me like a lunatic and knocked me over. I got up and went after him, but I was always behind him. Couldn't see anything

214

ahead. Then, just as I was catching up to him, he slipped over. I couldn't stop, so I tripped over him. When we got up, there was this gust of wind, kicked up some snow. So there was like a mini blizzard for a second or two. Couldn't see a thing. When it died down—"

"He'd gone," said Cole. "I went off in the direction he'd . . . toward where I thought I'd seen him . . ." His voice trailed off. And then he said: "I'm scared." He sounded just like a child.

And I knew how he felt.

When we finally abandoned our cold cups of tea, Ambler tried to persuade us to go back out. Cole and I didn't disagree with him; we just didn't say anything at all. And we didn't move. Well, Ambler lost his temper then, which I'd never seen him do before, I don't think. He shouted at us, pleaded with us, shouted at us again. He said if there was just a chance that the others might still be alive then we had to look for them.

By this point, Cole was sitting on the floor in the rec room, his back against the wall, hugging his knees. His eyes were squeezed shut and he was rocking ever so slightly backward and forward. I thought maybe he was right: maybe he was going mad. And just then, it seemed like a pretty attractive idea to me. Ambler finally gave up on us and headed out on his own. As if he didn't know what kind of story this is.

You don't go out alone.

I *should* have tried to stop him. I could just hear the engine of his ski-doo as he rode off. Cole was still on

215

the floor, rocking and mumbling; I couldn't bear to be near him. Went through to the dorm and climbed into my bunk. I burrowed down into my sleeping bag, got my head right in, and I shut my eyes tight. I wanted it to be dark. I wanted to sleep and make the world go away for a while. But it was still too light, and my head was too full of questions and fear, so I sat up, shaking up Jenny's snow globe, watching the water clear as the white flecks settled to the bottom, then shaking it up again, over and over.

In the end, I went back through to the rec room. Cole was in the same spot, but at least he'd stopped rocking now. He looked up at me as I walked in. Blank eyes. Blank face. I didn't like how he looked, and I wondered if I looked any better. I persuaded him to play a video game with me. Video games weren't really my thing, especially the ones Cole liked, but I wanted something to do with my hands, something unreal to occupy my mind. Literally to *occupy* my mind. To take up all the space in it and push everything else out.

So we spent two hours, three hours, four, shooting and slicing and blowing up zombies, till we must have started to look like them ourselves. And we died, and we died, and we died.

When I accidentally blew us both up by bouncing a grenade off a wall and straight back at us, I got up to go to the bathroom.

Cole said: "Get food."

"OK," I said.

As I headed out of the door, Cole was standing, stretching, yawning. He glanced out of the window. "No sign of Ambler," he said flatly.

I found all the worst foods in the kitchen and piled up platefuls of delicious unhealthiness for us both: cookies, cake, chocolate, potato chips. Like food for a child's party but without the little triangular sandwiches. Then I carried them slowly and carefully, like a tightrope walker, back to the rec room, concentrating hard on not dropping anything. I was shivering with cold before I got back but I refused to ask myself why.

The rec room was empty. The game console had come unplugged from the TV and the screen was full of white noise, like a snowstorm.

I heard the plates smashing at my feet, waking me from my daze. I ran to the window. There was Cole, wandering out over the ice, walking like a zombie. No coat, no boots. And there was a little squall of snow blown up just ahead of him: a twirling dance of snowflakes that he was walking straight into. And for a moment there seemed to be a small shadow ahead of him, a darker shape in the blizzard of white. Hard to see at that distance, and through the swirl of snow, but it looked like a boy.

I was stock-still, transfixed, with a weird tension building within me: a pressure and a sense of panic. I realized I was holding my breath, had been for too long. I breathed out, and the window steamed up in front of my face, blocking my view.

When I wiped it clean they were gone.

No boy. No Cole.

No swirling snow.

Just miles and miles of icy nothingness.

And only me in it now.

I looked out at it wearily. Eventually a shiver shook me alert enough to close the door. Good idea. Shut everything out. If I sat tight, then the main base would send someone out for me eventually. Wouldn't they?

If they were still there.

I slumped back down, close in front of the TV, and stared hard at the snowstorm of static on the screen. The random dancing pattern was soothing and hypnotic. I turned the volume up and the crackle and fizz that went with it drowned out the sound of the wind that was picking up outside, the sound of snow whipped up by the wind, hitting hard against the window.

There wasn't normally snow. There shouldn't have been snow, not in the coldest desert on earth. No snow. It was wrong. But at least I couldn't hear it now. And if I didn't look up from the screen then I wouldn't accidentally look out of the window. Wouldn't accidentally see the boy in the snowstorm, walking this way.

I put one hand into the pocket of my fleece and felt the toy in there, the snow globe. Wrapped my fingers around the smooth glass and thought of my sister, thought about home.

Distracted, my focus slipped and the TV snow blurred away to reveal the reflection of my face, haggard and gray and hollow-eyed. Then I focused again and my face dropped back behind the curtain of swirling white flecks, and I stared into it, and I listened to the static.

I didn't hear the outer door opening. And I didn't feel the icy rush of wind. I didn't hear footsteps in the corridor. I turned the TV up to full volume. Loud enough to hurt.

I stared at the screen.

I stared into the swirling white madness.

And then I closed my eyes and waited for the darkness.

And I wasn't afraid.

*J*ack's chest feels tight. He realizes, eventually, that
this is partly because his arms are wrapped around
his body, as if he's hugging himself for warmth, though
he can't tell how much of the cold he feels is real, and
how much has seeped into him from Mr. Randolph's
story. Either way, when he untangles his arms and the
tension remains, he wonders for a moment why that is.
Then he notices that he is holding his breath. He lets
out a small sigh of air and the tension subsides a little,
though the cold remains, and his breath paints a
candlelit smear of mist in the darkness.

He looks at Mr. Randolph, who squeezes his eyes
shut again, blinking away a subtle tension in his face to
regain his natural blank expression. He sits there, still
and straight and cold as ice, though no mist plays
around his thin lips, so far as Jack can see. This ought
to worry him, he realizes. In fact, a lot of things
ought to be worrying him now.

Because at some point during Mr. Randolph's story,
Jack accepted the inevitable truth of his situation. In
fact, he must have known for quite some time; he just
hadn't fully admitted it to himself. But now that he
has, he's a little surprised that he doesn't feel more
scared. He is scared, of course. He can feel the fear
inside him, trembling with potential. But somehow
he feels removed from it. The fear is just a fact, an
inevitable part of him that he feels and observes and

examines with quiet fascination. It's beyond his control, but it's not overwhelming. Not yet.

"Thank you, Mr. Randolph," says the pale man, and Mr. Randolph, without a word, nor even a hint of an emotion, blows out his candle and pushes back his chair.

Jack's heart is racing, and his mind is, too. Thoughts and ideas and fears are churning in his head. He stares down at the flame dancing on his stump of a candle; he concentrates, trying to steady himself, the mist of his breath mingling with the twisting ribbon of smoke. He swallows down a mouthful of cold air and raises his head again. Mr. Osterley's face is the only one Jack can make out at all now, a pale moon shining in the darkness.

Mr. Osterley is still and quiet for a long moment. At last, however, he raises a hand, palm upward, in Jack's direction, and smiles. At least, Jack thinks he smiles, or perhaps it is only the way the jittering light from the candle is playing on his face.

Jack readies himself to speak, wondering if the lump in his throat will allow any words past at all.

But then the pale man says: "You shall have the privilege of the final turn, Jack."

He lowers his hand, the stuttering light of his dying candle splintering its slow, smooth movement into jagged lurches as it reunites with the other in a loose embrace before him.

"First, I shall tell my own story."

Among the Dead

My name is Frederick William Osterley. In life I was an undertaker. I lived my life among the dead. My father was an undertaker, too, and I was born into the trade. I mean this quite literally. My mother went into labor in the mortuary of the family business while my father, unaware, discussed coffin choices with two recently bereaved sisters in his office above. My mother gave birth to me there in the mortuary, with the minimum of fuss and no noise, concerned as she was not to further distress my father's grieving customers. According to her, I followed her example and did not cry until after they had safely departed. I was three weeks early. It was the first and last time I ever demonstrated impatience.

My father, it was said, had a face for undertaking. His features, at rest, naturally arranged themselves into a picture of somber mournfulness, which was a great asset in his chosen profession. He looked the part, and so customers were content to put their trust in him. And they were right to do so: he was conscientious, hardworking, and had a natural sympathy for the pain of others. He saw people at their lowest ebb: broken, crazed, angry, and he treated them only with respect, courtesy, and immense care. He was quite masterful at his trade, but thought little about it. Mostly he was content to know that his work gave some comfort to his customers in their darkest days, even if many of them failed to appreciate this. Many times I saw customers turn their anger toward him, occasionally they even struck him, but my father never bore them any ill will.

"We see them to their rest," he calmly told me once, holding a handkerchief to his recently bloodied nose. "The living *and* the dead: we see them to their rest."

I began to work with him at a young age. Menial tasks at first: polishing coffins, cleaning, and other small chores and errands. Then, as my schooling progressed, I helped my mother with the paperwork and bookkeeping. Then, later still, I worked with the clients. This was how my father termed them: our customers were the living; our clients were the dead.

"The clients are a lot less trouble than the customers," he told me once. "But the customers pay the bills."

I was not yet thirteen when I began to help with our clients, but I still had very little to do with our customers for many years after that. I had picked up the technical side of the business with ease. I learned how to prepare a body for burial or cremation, and learned the science and craft of embalming. I could even, in the rare instances where it was required, reconstruct the likeness of the deceased to even the most badly injured faces. I had, if I say so myself, a rare talent for the dead.

But not so with the living. I lacked my father's natural advantages in the business. My face did not possess the same delicate balance of features. Where he looked solemn and trustworthy, I seemed cold and aloof. And though, as time passed, I learned to imitate the care he showed to our customers, I had no understanding of their feelings, their pain. I did not understand loss. I knew all about death, or so I thought, but nothing at all about grief.

In fact, I knew little about anything much outside of the tiny world of our house and the work we did. Throughout my schooldays I was an awkward child and made few friends, and my father's profession made me an easy target for mockery and bullying. So I took refuge in my home life. And we were a happy family, in our way. My father may have worn a permanent expression of deep sadness, and my mother could seldom be tempted out of silence, but we were contented with our lot, and we knew amongst ourselves that this was understood. We devoted ourselves to one another and to our work, and we drew strength from our sense of belonging and from the knowledge that we were doing good.

And then my father died.

My father died and he taught me the last thing I needed to know about our dismal profession. He made me understand. I felt the loss of him keenly. My mother, too, of course, though again all emotion and distress was carefully hidden from our customers. My father had died suddenly but discreetly after completing his duties at the funeral of a Mr. Oliver Withinshaw.

Mr. Withinshaw's widow had been distraught and had to be restrained from climbing down into her husband's grave to join him, but my father had whispered calming words to her and led her away. The wake was a dignified affair and passed without incident. My father, satisfied that all was well, departed early.

He died quietly at the kitchen table shortly after arriving home, sitting up straight, his hands one on top of the other on the table in front of him, his eyes closed. His heart, emptied by years of selfless compassion, simply stopped. His undertaker's face, oddly, looked less mournful in death than it had in life. When I found him there, he looked more peaceful and contented than I had ever seen him.

Those unfamiliar and confusing emotions that my mother and I felt at this time we held in check. We were professional and maintained appearances for the sake of ourselves and each other, and for the business. We arranged my father's funeral, and we sent him to his rest, and we took comfort in the pride he would have taken in seeing the thing done right. And though we now carried a sea of sorrow inside, we would not let it flood out and drown us. Instead, we held it safe within ourselves. The morning after my father's funeral I saw a little more of his likeness in my reflection when I shaved.

*

Life went on, and so did our business. With my father gone, my mother and I had much more contact with the customers. But I was ready for that now. I held within me my own grief, and it gave me understanding. I spoke to our customers with a new authority, and I took a part of their sorrows from them and added it to my own. And I sent the living and the dead to their rest. I did it well, and for many years. It was all of my life.

My mother made occasional halfhearted inquiries about whether I might ever settle down and have a family of my own, but neither of us, I think, ever considered it a real possibility. I felt no need or want for such a thing. I played my part in the world well enough alone, and I knew too well the eventual fate of all living things. Besides, I had no wish to share my life with anyone. It was not a life that would suit another, I thought. And most of all, I did not wish to share my grief. Now that I had found it, I held it close. It had become an exquisite pain inside of me, a precious, delicious thing. I had spent so long feeling so little, and now, invisible to the world, I held a storm of darkness within me. It was agony and delight at once. Do not expect to understand; I did not. But somehow, I felt, that grief was my father's gift to me, and I guarded it jealously.

In time, of course, my mother gave me more. Thirty years after my father's death, after an illness just long enough for us to prepare ourselves, she left this world.

When the time came, she bade me farewell with as little fuss, and as much strength, as she had demonstrated at my birth. She said: "Good-bye, my child," closed her eyes, and was gone.

She had arranged the funeral herself, and it was a quiet masterpiece. Nothing extravagant, but everything perfectly correct. We did it well, as you would expect. I was the model of professionalism, as she would have wished, and spoke sincerely of her contribution to the business throughout her life. I did not speak of her as a mother. She would have thought it unseemly.

I could tell you of the years following that, but there is little point. I served my purpose on the earth for another seventeen years and then I, too, left it. I had carried on the legacy of my father faithfully, I believe. I had sent many hundreds of the living and the dead to their rest, and I had done it well.

But when *I* died, there was no one to send me to mine. Of course there was a funeral, carefully prepared and run with perfect precision by the small staff that I had left behind; able men and well trained. They did it competently enough. It was organized and efficient, but it was hardly a challenge. I had made it easy for them after all. There was no one to console. There was a funeral, but there were no mourners. Oh, it was well enough attended, and I was shown due respect, but none truly grieved my passing. No one really cared, and why should they? Why would the living care about my death, when my own life had been devoted only to the dead? I cannot begrudge them their indifference. So my life ended unremarked upon, and that was an end to it.

Only, then, death was not the end. Then there was *this*. I was dead, but not gone. I was a ghost, a spirit, a wandering soul; whatever fanciful name you prefer to give to this odd state. And I found that there were others like me, others who persisted in this half-life. Others who had failed properly to depart.

Some are confused, some angry, some lost. Each, for whatever reason, cannot yet accept their fate. So I gather them together, and they tell their stories, and it eases them a little. In due course they will go on—do not ask me where—and others will take their place.

I am Frederick William Osterley and in death, as in life, I am among the dead.

And I help them to their rest.

M r. Osterley blinks once slowly. Then he meets Jack's eyes with his impassive, unreadable gaze, just for a moment before he bows toward the ailing flame of his candle, blows it out, and his face dissolves into the thick black.

Jack is alone now in a fragile pool of wavering light, staring out into the boundless dark as if he is floating in space. The others must still be out there, but his candle's weak glow cannot reach them.

Not long left for that flame now. Not long left for that last glimmer of light. Not long until the end of all this, whatever that might turn out to be.

He takes in a measured breath, holds it for a second. He is scared, of course. But he is ready now. He doesn't know everything that he is going to say, but at least he knows how he will begin.

"I'm not dead," he says. "Is that all right?"

The House
Where the
Ghosts Meet

I've been dreading this. I didn't have a story to tell you, you see, not when I came in, at least. So I've been sitting here this whole time wondering what I could say when it was my turn. I was trying to think if there was anything I'd ever read or seen on TV that I could use, but I knew that'd be no good. And besides, I'm rubbish at telling other people's stories like that. I always get it all wrong and tell it in the wrong order and miss out a bit near the beginning that you really need to know for the end to make sense. Things like that. So I knew that that was no good. And I still didn't know what to say until just now.

Right just now I realized what I would have to say.

You see, there's this house. It's not very far from where I live, but it's not on the way to the shops or the swimming pool or any of my friends' houses, so I never used to go past it very often. But I've noticed it whenever I have gone by. It's bigger and older than any of the other houses around here, and it seems as if it's been empty for a long while. And that's a bit odd, I suppose, but I never really thought about it much.

And then, a while ago, somebody—I don't remember who—told me it was haunted. Actually, hang on, that's not quite true. What they said was that it was haunted, but only for one night each year: that there was this one night, the same date each year, when ghosts came to the house. They made it sound like it was a club or something.

Of course, I didn't believe them. I knew there was no such thing as ghosts. I thought they were joking, so I took no notice. Only, well, I suppose I must have taken some notice, mustn't I? Because I remembered it. And I kept thinking about it whenever I went by. And after that I did find myself going past more often. Not deliberately, you understand; it's just that I started going to a couple of places that were in the area, and it was the natural route to take. More or less. Just coincidence. And as I was passing by anyway, I did sometimes take a glance at the house, and I thought: Well, it doesn't *look* like a haunted house, not really. Not like they do in films and on TV. It was just a house. Oh, and it's got a TV antenna, which doesn't seem right for a haunted house somehow, does it? You don't think of ghosts sitting around watching television.

"Shh! Stop rattling your chains! I'm trying to watch EastEnders!*"*

Anyway . . .

I decided it wasn't haunted, obviously; it was just empty. But I still kept looking at it when I went by. And now sometimes I went by even when I didn't need to. And I wanted to ask whoever it was who'd said it was haunted why they'd said that. Whether it was a joke or if it was something they'd been told by somebody else.

236

But I just couldn't remember who it had been. Anyway, I told myself it was all just silly. There was no reason to think it was haunted, not really. There wasn't really anything especially interesting about it at all, so I told myself I'd stop looking, that I'd avoid going down that road completely.

So that's what I did. And it worked. I forgot all about the stupid unhaunted house.

Until tonight.

I don't know why I'm here.

I just wandered down the road without really thinking about it, and the point where I realized I was walking entirely the wrong way and stopped in my tracks was when I was right outside the house. And that's when I saw the light.

Just a thin line of light at one window, where the curtains weren't quite closed properly. And not a steady light. It was flickering, so I thought it must be either candles or a fire. So I wondered who was in there. And there was a gap in the fence that I thought I could just about get through.

So I did. And I'm not brave. Or stupid, actually. Not usually, anyway. But I went through the hole in the fence, and I thought I could hear voices, maybe, when I was under the window. And then I felt a bit foolish because what was I going to do then? I wasn't going to knock on the door. I wasn't going to throw a brick through the window and climb in. But while I thought about it I walked around to the back of the house in

237

case anyone looked out of the window and saw me. And the back door was open.

I told myself I should just go home. I still don't know why I didn't. But I didn't. I went in, and I crept through to the foot of the stairs in the dark. Oh, and every time the floorboards creaked I stopped and listened and thought about running away again. But I wanted to know what was going on. I suppose I wanted just to prove to myself that there was a sensible explanation, that the house wasn't haunted.

So I went up the stairs. It was really dark going up there, so that was scary. And the stairs were creakier than the floorboards downstairs, so that made it even scarier. But once I was up on the landing there was a bit more light, because there was half a moon shining through a window at the end of the hallway. And it was easy enough to see which door I was after because, of course, there was a little line of light under it: the same flickering light as I'd seen at the window. So I went over to it and listened. And there *were* voices, but I couldn't really make out any words, even when I pressed my ear against the door.

And that really frustrated me. I still didn't think it was ghosts in the room, obviously. But I wanted to see for myself, to prove it, to prove wrong the person— who I still couldn't even remember who it was—who'd made up the ridiculous story in the first place. And then, oh yes, the door handle was really cold! I hadn't even realized I'd been reaching for it, so I nearly squealed with surprise at the shock of it being so cold. Then I just stood there very still, for ages and ages, with my hand on the door handle, telling myself what a stupid idea it would be to go in, what a stupid idea it was even to be there in the first place. I told myself to go home. I told myself over and over.

Then I turned the handle, and I went in.

I came in.

I came in and saw you all. And you weren't ghosts, so that was a relief. Only it wasn't, because of course I'd already known that anyway. No such thing. And it also wasn't a relief because if you weren't ghosts, then that just meant I was in a room in a deserted house with twelve total strangers who might all be serial killers for all I know.

No offense.

And I still didn't know why I was here. And I didn't know why you were here. But I wanted to find out, so I took a seat, and kept myself ready to make a run for it if I needed to, and I watched and I listened.

And you started telling your stories.

They frightened me. I mean, they frightened me even more than I was already frightened. And they frightened me not just because they were scary stories but because I believed them. I believed them because I could tell that *you* believed them. No, not just believed them; you knew that they *were* true. You *knew* it. And I suppose at some point I realized why.

Because there *are* such things as ghosts after all,

aren't there? But the odd thing is, when I realized, when I finally admitted to myself that you are all . . . that you're . . . ghosts, that you're all dead—that I was in a room full of dead people—when I realized *that*, it didn't actually make me any more scared, I don't think. But it did make me wonder again why you're here. Why would ghosts tell each other ghost stories?

But I worked it out. At least, I think I worked it out. Here's what I think . . .

This is the house where the ghosts meet. To tell stories. To tell *ghost* stories. You come to tell your stories, and you try to scare each other. And you all hope that you'll *be* scared. You hope to feel afraid. And alive. Because that's kind of when you feel *most* alive, isn't it? When you're afraid. That's a thrill when you're alive, isn't it? So I suppose, maybe, it's even more of a thrill when you're dead. To be reminded of life when your own life is over. To remember what it's like to feel your heart beating fast in your chest.

And, well, I don't think I can do that. I don't think I can scare you with a story. But maybe I can help you remember what it's like. Life. Because my heart is beating now. You don't notice it most of the time, of course—you're concentrating on other things and your heart's just quietly going about its business, not making a fuss. But now that I'm scared, now that I'm properly scared, I can feel it racing and rattling inside me. And my breath . . . I've been trying not to let it show, but it's been feeling like the most complicated thing in the world just to breathe. It's so difficult. How have I managed it for so long without thinking about it?

But oh, the air! The air is so delicious! I am terrified, and I can barely make my lungs work, but . . . I am tasting every breath, and it's amazing. Sweet, beautiful air. This room is full of breath and I'm drinking it down.

And this feeling now, it's like . . . what is it like? It's like . . .

Oh, I know. On vacation with my parents at the seaside and walking along the path at the top of the cliffs, and there was a butterfly . . . well, there were loads of butterflies, mostly those red ones—I can't remember what they're called. But this was a different one, a blue one like I hadn't seen before, and it just flitted past my head as I was walking along behind Mum and Dad. I only just glimpsed it; it was just this blue blur out of the corner of my eye, and it disappeared down into the gorse and the grass at the side of the path. And I just wanted a closer look at it, so I went after it, off the path, head down, looking for it.

And I couldn't see it, and I couldn't see it . . .

And then all of a sudden there it is, right in front of me, bright summer sun on its wings, and I bend down and look at it close-up, really close, and the light picks out every detail. I look at it really close and it's so beautiful and so strange, and its wings look so fragile and precious, and its head looks like something from another planet, and its body is all sort of hairy. And it's just amazing, and I'm leaning in even closer to see more, and it's like I'm in sort of a trance. It's like nothing else exists, just this tiny, delicate, brilliant, weird, beautiful thing.

Then all of a sudden it flaps its wings and takes off straight into my face, and I go "Ah!" and I jump up and step back, but my foot hits a root or something and I lose my balance and start to tip over backward. So then I put my other foot back to steady myself.

But only the front of it lands on anything.

My toe is on the cliff but there's nothing under my heel. And I'm right on the edge of the cliff. And I'm still off balance.

And I gasp in some air and it feels like it fills up my whole body. Like suddenly every bit of me is all tense and tight and tingling. Like my whole body is holding my breath. Then I put my weight forward, take half a step, and spin myself around and stand there, toes right up against the edge, and I look down.

A long, long way down. And rocks at the bottom. And there's this wheezing noise as I pull in even more breath. I feel like a balloon blown up as far as it can go, only just not bursting—my chest is straining trying to hold it in. And just for a second, I feel what it would be like.

I feel the fall, down to the rocks, the rush of air, feel myself hurtling and twisting down, feel this rushing, rattling, buzzing feeling inside me, like a swarm of bees. Feel the wind rushing up over me. I feel my body screaming. And it's all just too much and my legs start to go all wobbly, and I know, I just know, that I'm going to faint. I'm going to tip forward and *really* fall. I'm going to fall. I'm going to fall from a great height, incredibly fast, onto rocks.

I'm going to die. I'm going to die. I'm going to die. And even when I've taken two steps back and I'm perfectly safe and everything is fine, and I've checked that my parents didn't see me and aren't going to tell me off for being so stupid, even then I'm still full of that feeling. That fear. That thrill. And I think I could have died. I could have died, but I didn't. And I am the most alive I have ever been.

And I feel the beating of my heart. And I taste my breath.

Do you remember? Can you remember what that's like? I think you probably can.

I hope so.

Jack feels as if he's been running. He's not much of a talker usually, but once he got going he found that the words just tumbled out, bundling and barging out of him like an unruly crowd. It was thrilling, like a fairground ride, and at the end of it he is breathless, exhausted, and light-headed.

He stretches his head back and blows out a long breath while his heart thumps away in his chest. Then he drops his head forward and squints into the darkness, searching for the faintest hint of the pale man's face, but finding nothing. The dim light from the dying flame of his candle barely even picks out his own hands there on the tabletop, so faintly visible that he might be the only one able to see how much they are trembling. He thinks that the others are still there but they make no sound, and he can no longer see a single one of them. Even looking around for his nearest neighbors, closest to the failing candlelight, he finds no sign. If they are there then the flame's shrinking glow cannot reach them.

Jack wouldn't have thought that being surrounded by dead people could ever provide any comfort, but now he wishes he could see them all rather than feeling alone in the embrace of this unnatural darkness.

He feels suddenly enormously tired, as if he has been awake for days, like the man in Mr. Blackmore's story.

His eyelids droop, and his eyes drop to the tiny stub of his candle. It has burned down almost to nothingness, a smear of wax and a blink of fire. He watches it for a moment, dreamily fascinated that it can still burn. Surely any moment now it will be gone. Any moment now.

Now, to his right, he hears a faint, low sound, too quiet to place. Perhaps just the kind of noise that any old house might make in dark silence. Or perhaps the softest creak of a floorboard trodden upon. Perhaps Mr. Osterley has risen from his seat.

Jack turns his head to look, but now the flame finally stutters out, and the last ember of light is swallowed up by the deep darkness . . .

Jack closes his eyes.

He doesn't know what will happen next. He doesn't know how this will end. Perhaps he ought to run.

But Jack is a curious boy.

*M*egan looks up at the old house, scowling at the crack of light in the upstairs window. It's nonsense of course, what that boy told her about this place. What was his name anyway? James? Josh? Something beginning with J, she thinks. She can't really remember much about him at all. Strange little kid. It must be nearly a year now since he told her. What had he called this place? The House Where the Ghosts Meet. That was it.

Silly little idiot.

Just ridiculous.

Still, she wonders if there's a way in around the back.

Acknowledgments

With thanks to:
Bella Pearson for editing, cheerleading, and wisdom;
David Fickling for patience and faith;
Ness Wood for designing, general brilliance,
and moral support;
Sue Cook for copyediting
(especially her vital tidying of errant punctuation);
Pam Smy for, you know, everything;
and Mila Bartolomé Smy for inspiration
and musical accompaniment.